FUTURE HERO

SCHOLASTIC

SPECIAL THANKS TO
ISAAC HAMILTON-MCKENZIE AND JASMINE RICHARDS

Published in the UK by Scholastic, 2024
1 London Bridge, London, SE1 9BG
Scholastic Ireland, 89E Lagan Road, Dublin Industrial Estate,
Glasnevin, Dublin, D11 HP5F

SCHOLASTIC and associated logos are trademarks and/or
registered trademarks of Scholastic Inc.

Text © Storymix Limited, 2024
Illustrations © Deise Lino, 2024
Cover illustration © Alicia Robinson, 2024

The right of Storymix Limited to be identified
as the author of this work has been asserted by them under
the Copyright, Designs and Patents Act 1988.

ISBN 978 0702 31184 0

A CIP catalogue record for this book is available from the British Library.

Printed and bound in Great Britain by Clays Ltd, Elcograf S.p.A

Paper made from wood grown in sustainable forests
and other controlled sources.

MIX
Paper | Supporting
responsible forestry
FSC® C018072
www.fsc.org

1 3 5 7 9 10 8 6 4 2

REMI BLACKWOOD

FUTURE HERO

BATTLE FOR SKY KINGDOM

ILLUSTRATED BY ALICIA ROBINSON AND DEISE LINO

■ SCHOLASTIC

To Jasmine. My mentor, and very own Legsy – thank you for your faith and guidance!

– IHM

For the readers. For the champions. For all those on the quest with me. **– JR**

CHAPTER ONE

LOOKING REAL SHARP

"C'mon, Jarell, look alive. Stop daydreaming!" Dad urged.

Jarell gave up trying to loosen his collar in the car-door window and hurried to his family waiting for him at the crossing.

Nasty outfit, Jarell thought as his new shoes pinched angrily at his toes. It was bad enough

wearing school uniform all week, but wearing a jacket and a shirt with a collar on a Saturday? Ugh. Why did Omari insist on "dapper" as the dress code for this party? Dapper according to who?

As soon as we get to Fades for Uncle Malcolm's party, this jacket is coming off, Jarell decided. *As soon as Mum gets distracted, of course.* He kicked an almost empty drinks can into the gutter. His feet in the new shoes did not appreciate it. *Ouch!*

Lucas grinned at him. Somehow his older brother looked stylish no matter what he wore. It wasn't fair.

"This jacket is too tight," Jarell complained. "And so are the shoes."

His mum glanced at him. "Looks good to me!" she said as the lights at the crossing turned green. "Now hurry up."

"Bro, you're walking like an old man," Lucas teased as they crossed the road. "No wonder we're late."

Jarell felt like punching his brother in the arm. "Quit blaming me!" he exclaimed.

If his dad hadn't forgotten to buy Uncle Malcolm a birthday card, they would have reached Fades ages ago. Instead they had to stop and get one on the way. It's not like they hadn't had plenty of warning. Omari had sent out invites as soon as

Uncle Malcolm announced his visit from Jamaica six weeks ago. For once, it wasn't Jarell's fault they were late.

"I don't even look like myself," Jarell said as he caught a glimpse of his reflection in the mobile phone shop window.

His mum turned and fixed his lapels. "You look great, as smooth as cocoa butter!" She glanced at his dad. "It's a shame your father didn't dress up. No one else at his brother's party will be wearing a tracksuit! Omari said 'dapper'."

"Jackets don't suit me!" Dad said defensively. "I don't understand why you're making such a big deal out of this anyway, Alesha."

Jarell's mum tutted. "I switched shifts with two other bus drivers so we could come to this party together. Aren't you excited to see your brother after all this time?"

Jarell knew it must have been a while because he only had vague memories of Uncle Malcolm running Fades before handing the barbershop over to his son Omari. Jarell couldn't imagine not seeing his brother Lucas for longer than a week, even if he was annoying.

His dad waved his hand. "I love my big brother. And I'm grateful he looks after Momma and Poppa, but *jeez*, he's like a broken record. If I have to hear about the motherland and his new-found spiritual connection to his roots one more time—" Myles took in a deep breath. "Not all of us are chasing adventure. I'm happy right where I am – with my family."

Jarell loved his family too, but he also ached to return to the ancient-future realm of Ulfrika. He never felt more alive than when he was there having adventures – even when he was searching in the stifling heat of Fire Mountain, or swimming through the murky Shadow Sea, or fighting zombie-like creatures in the underground City of Clay. At first, Jarell hadn't thought it was possible that he was the heir of Kundi – the long-awaited Future Hero who would save Ulfrika from the evil sorcerer Ikala – but he was starting to believe it could be true. His adventures had changed him. *Does this mean I'm turning into Uncle Malcolm?* he wondered.

The joyful boom of old dance-hall music and the buzz of voices greeted them as they turned on to the high street. Most of the shops were closed and Malcolm's party had spilled out on to the pavement in front of Fades. Strings of fairy lights sparkled outside the barbershop, and somewhere inside, a disco ball scattered shards of rainbow colour everywhere. Everyone was dressed to the nines. A wave of excitement rushed over Jarell. *People are going to be talking about this party for weeks.*

Jarell's cousin Omari looked pretty stressed as he greeted them at the door. He didn't look comfortable in his jacket either. It made Jarell feel a bit better.

"Uncle, Auntie, how are we, family?" Omari said, bringing everyone into an embrace. "You guys look sharp!" His eyes flickered over Jarell's dad pretty quickly.

"The party looks great," said Myles with a smile, peering into the barbershop. "And what is that I smell?" Myles smacked his lips. "It must be Red's cooking."

Omari chuckled. "You've got a good nose, Unc. Red's catering with his dad Winston. We've got everything from curried goat and fried chicken, to plantain and patties. Get stuck in."

"It would be rude not to," Dad replied, rubbing his hands together. He skipped into Fades without another word, followed by Lucas.

Mum shook her head. "I promise you, Omari, we didn't just come for the food," she said, following them inside.

Omari laughed, then brushed Jarell's shoulder. "I don't think I've seen you look so dapper, cuz. You clean up nice!"

"Thanks." Jarell smiled. "Dad's right, the party looks great."

"I hope so, it's been proper stressful to organize." Omari rubbed his neck, something Jarell's cousin only did when he was in for a nightmare haircut. The pressure must be unreal. "I just wanted to give my pops a good impression, you know? Show him how well I'm taking care of the shop. How well we're doing."

"Fades is always packed," Jarell said. "It's like the heart of the neighbourhood."

"You flatter me, cuz." Omari smiled.

Suddenly, with the ear-splitting sound of a scratch, the music stopped. A chorus of protests erupted from everyone dancing. Jarell caught sight of his brother plugging his phone into the decks. Lucas flashed a cheeky grin as the "Candy" song dropped and cheers replaced the complaints. Everyone dancing started forming lines, stepping and swaying together in perfect sync.

If it weren't for the fact that he was still in plain view of his mum, Jarell would have been tempted to take off his jacket and join in.

"C'mon, get yourself a drink," Omari said cheerfully, dragging him inside. Jarell poured himself a glass of Red's famous holiday punch, a secret blend of fruit juice and spices that had an almost lava-like red glow.

He tucked himself behind his parents, out of

the way of the grown-ups hitting the dance floor. He sipped the punch, the flavours transporting him to a beach somewhere at sunset. *I wish Kimisi could taste this*, he thought. *It would blow her mind.* Although, knowing his warrior and griot friend, she would probably spend time asking why it was called "punch" and might even demonstrate the force of her own strike.

"Yuh arrived!" someone bellowed, pushing through the dancers. Uncle Malcolm wore a fitted light grey suit and gold rings on eight of his ten fingers. His skin was glowing with health and rest. Jarell couldn't lie, his uncle was the one that looked as smooth as cocoa butter.

"Wahgwan, family!" Uncle Malcolm grinned, taking them all in for a hug. "Thanks for coming."

"We wouldn't miss it," said Alesha. "And doesn't Fades look great?"

Uncle Malcolm frowned slightly. Omari, who was close by, looked stricken as he saw his dad's face. Jarell really felt for his cousin.

"Is something wrong?" Myles asked.

"It's just ... I didn't realize my taste was so out of style," Uncle Malcolm replied.

Omari looked to the heavens. "We've been through this already, Pops. The water leak ruined everything – I had no choice but to change it."

Uncle Malcolm chuckled. "Mi know, son. I'm teasin' and I'm proud of you." He grabbed Omari and squeezed his face. "Anyways, I know more than most about the benefits of change. Everyone thought I was a fool, picking up sticks and moving back 'a yard. They warned me the Jamaica now isn't the one that our parents left decades ago. But when I touch that grass, walk among the trees and hike to di top a di Blue Mountains, I feel at home! I see my ancestors in the stars. Nothing more beautiful than that."

Jarell saw his dad roll his eyes at Uncle Malcolm's speech and tuck into a piece of fried chicken.

"Mi see that, brother!" Uncle Malcolm jabbed him. "All I'm saying is, sometimes yuh have to give up what yuh know to gain something more. The worl' is so much bigger than South London."

If only you knew that our ancestors came from another universe before they arrived in this dimension, thought Jarell. What would his uncle make of being descended from the great Ulfrikan warrior king, Kundi? The heaviness of that knowledge weighed on his shoulders. Jarell knew his family were not ready for that truth, and it would be unsafe for them to know while the sorcerer Ikala was on the loose.

"How did I miss these?" Uncle Malcolm said, pointing to the framed drawings on the wall. Jarell held his breath – not everyone liked his futuristic artwork, and no one except Legsy knew that they were of a real place, Ulfrika.

Omari grinned at Jarell. "They're nice, huh? The artist is none other than—"

"They look like they cost a fortune!" Uncle

Malcolm exclaimed. "You spending all your money on paintings, son?"

"Not a penny," Omari said defiantly. "Jarell did them."

The whole family turned to stare at Jarell as if he were famous. The hairs on the back of Jarell's neck prickled against the stiff shirt collar. He wasn't sure celebrity status was for him.

"Is that right?" Uncle Malcolm breathed. "What a talent in our family!"

"The next Kehinde Wiley," Jarell's dad said, giving him a hug. Even Lucas looked *almost* proud.

"Defo," Omari added. "People love his work. His paintings are practically all the customers ask about ... other than my cuts."

Suddenly, Jarell spotted the razor-thin frame of Legsy slicing through the crowd. In a sharp charcoal suit, the trickster god looked more like a local businessman than an Ancient from another world.

"Legsy," Jarell called excitedly, but when Legsy turned in his direction his normally mischievous eyes were filled with worry.

CHAPTER TWO

A TRUST BETRAYED

The Ancient cut across the dance floor without breaking eye contact with Jarell. Whatever was on his mind, Legsy looked properly spooked. But before Legsy could tell him anything, Jarell's dad had snared the trickster god with an arm around the shoulder.

Don't ask for a haircut, Jarell groaned inside.

His dad had been banging on about Legsy being a "barber with the skills of a wizard" ever since he'd had his first trim with him.

"I need to see you soon, my friend," his dad told Legsy. "I can't have my son looking sharper than me."

"You always look pretty sharp, Myles," Legsy responded kindly. "But I've misplaced my logbook. Perhaps Jarell can help me find it?"

"I'd be happy to—" Jarell started, eager to help them get out of there.

"How about me?" Uncle Malcolm interrupted. "Could ya fit me in?"

Jarell bunched his fists in frustration. Legsy gave a weak smile. "Of course. Any time."

The music stopped abruptly and switched tracks.

"But wait … that's my song!" Uncle Malcolm was already heading off to dance.

Barber with the skills of a wizard is right, Jarell

thought wryly as Legsy flashed him a mischievous grin. *That just leaves Dad to get rid of.*

"Did anyone else try the plantain?" Jarell asked. "It was *so* good, but it's almost finished!"

His dad froze in mid-chew of the salt-fish patty he was munching. "How did I miss the plantain? Stay there, Legsy, I'll be right back." He hurried off muttering something about the price of plantain and it being a travesty.

Jarell and Legsy wasted no time, weaving through the dancers to the VIP room at the back of the barbershop.

"What's happened?" Jarell asked.

"Not here," Legsy replied, before vanishing through the colourful beaded curtain.

Jarell hesitated and glanced back. His father was two-stepping with a plate of fried plantain in his hand. His mother was laughing at the makeshift bar with her best friend Marcia. And, of course, Lucas was playing on the console with a cousin and a couple of his mates. *Can I really leave during a family party?*

Wasn't his home and family enough? Part of him wanted to be like his dad – happy knowing he was where he belonged. But there was a part of him that was more like Uncle Malcolm than he realized. Jarell knew he was the Future Hero. The people of Ulfrika needed him to fight Ikala. He was the only one who could stop the evil sorcerer from destroying both their worlds.

Jarell slipped through the beaded curtain into the VIP room, taking in the super-slick barber's chair and the shiny high-tech surfaces. His gaze went to the dark carved-wood frame of Legsy's mirror. It was part of the magic that allowed him to cross over into Ulfrika.

Jarell skimmed a hand across the back of his head. For the magic to work, his hair had to be long enough for Legsy to cut a magical symbol into it.

"It'll do," Legsy said as if just noticing him. He was rummaging through one of his drawers.

"What's got you so worried?" Jarell asked. "And what about the party? I can't bail on my family. Mum will kill me!"

Legsy gave the chair a quick brush and turned it around. Jarell sat down, staring at him expectantly. Legsy suddenly looked more than just older, he looked positively ancient. *This can't be good*, Jarell thought.

Legsy sighed. "It's the Iron Eagle; Ikala knows where it is and— And I'm not sure we can stop him."

Jarell felt ice crawl up his spine. Ayana, the Goddess of Storms and Rains, had scattered the four Iron Animals from the Staff of Kundi to protect it from Ikala. Jarell had promised to reunite them. In his quest to make the staff whole again, he had already found the Iron Leopard, the Iron Crocodile and the Iron Snake. Only the Iron Eagle eluded him. Without it, the staff would never be powerful enough to defeat Ikala.

"Ayana entrusted the Iron Eagle to the God of Thunder, Oufula," Legsy said. "She must have thought, because they were once married, that Oufula would keep it safe for her in Fekuk. But the God of Thunder hasn't got over the break-up. He's offering the Iron Eagle as the prize in a competition to find the greatest warrior in Ulfrika."

Jarell dug his fingernails into the arm of the chair. "But he can't! What if Ikala gets his hands on it?"

"The only way to stop him is for *you* to win," Legsy replied. He turned Jarell so he could see his reflection in the mirror and picked up the clippers. "*You* are the heir of Kundi – if anyone can beat Ikala in a competition, it's you. Now choose a symbol."

The shapes carved in the dark wooden frame of Legsy's mirror seemed different this time. Jarell couldn't see any of the patterns he'd used before. He snorted. It shouldn't have surprised him. The mirror was a mixture of advanced technology and powerful magic. It could see into the past, present and future, and gaze into other worlds.

Jarell trusted the mirror to guide him. He felt his eyes returning again and again to one special carving. A curving V-shape that was symmetrical and elegant with a texture that remind him of feathers. Jarell pointed to it.

"The wings," Legsy said. "A symbol of courage and unity. That knowing our strength comes not just from the belief we have in ourselves, but also from our trust in others."

Legsy's clippers hummed and weaved through Jarell's hair. But halfway through, the trickster god stopped. "How can I call myself the God of Doorways when I am trapped here? I should be with you to fight for the Iron Eagle."

After all this time, Jarell still didn't know why the trickster god had been banished from Ulfrika.

"If you tell me what happened, I could help you," Jarell replied.

Legsy shook his head, switching the clippers back on to avoid Jarell's gaze. "No. You would think less of me if you knew."

What does that mean? Jarell wondered. Legsy finished cutting. He brushed away the hair from Jarell's neck, then gently placed a hand on his shoulder. "Use what you see to your advantage, Jarell."

Legsy's Ulfrikan chant rose and fell like a bird of prey soaring on the wind. The wings carved into the ebony frame glowed and the mirror's surface rippled.

Jarell swallowed hard, his throat suddenly dry. *Could he really win a competition to find Ulfrika's greatest warrior?*

He reached out to the silvery surface of the

mirror. As he touched it, warm liquid raced up his arm. His itchy, ill-fitting party clothes were transformed into the sleek, collarless suit he wore in Ulfrika. The symbol in his hair started to burn and, in the blink of an eye, Jarell was falling through darkness.

*

Crunch!

Sharp gravel stabbed through the high-tech fabric covering his body. As Jarell tried to move, red dust the colour of ground chillies caught in the back of his throat. He coughed and his body shook, the needle-like stones jabbing harder against him.

Fighting against the pain, Jarell slowly got to his feet. He flicked off any gravel refusing to fall away. He'd been lucky not to break any bones, he realized, or worse, as he noticed the jagged sandstone stacks towering up across the valley floor.

He stepped carefully, stretching his bruised body. The sides of the valley rose into mountainous cliffs that framed a perfect sapphire-blue sky. Spurts of green shrubs peeked from small crevices, but other than that, it was starkly barren and beautiful.

Jarell wished he had his pencils – and the time to draw. But he needed to work out where he was and how to find the god Oufula as soon as possible.

A rumble of thunder rolled through the valley. The bright sunshine vanished. Graphite-grey clouds filled the sky with almost unnatural speed, followed by bold, fluorescent-yellow scars of lightning.

Jarell's high-tech suit suddenly jerked him back. Seconds later, a lump of ice the size of his fist smashed into the ground where he had been standing. Then another. Hailstones! Missiles of ice exploded against the rock around him, chilling the air.

Jarell raced to the side of the valley looking for shelter. The sound of ice drumming against stone was like the wildest movie soundtrack.

The wind picked up, chucking lumps of ice at him. Jarell could have sworn the hail was aiming for him. He dropped and rolled as if it was a giant game of dodgeball, weaving his way through the hail. His suit offered almost no protection from direct hits. He could feel bruises bloom on his body.

Got to get out of this, he told himself.

Scanning the bottom of the rock face as he ran, he spotted an overhang. *Quick!* He sprinted towards it, the hail thumping against his back, and slid into the cave.

Safe. Jarell bolted upright as he remembered that nothing in Ulfrika was as it seemed. *What else is sheltering with me?* Cautiously he checked the cave for snakes and scorpions. Only when he was as confident as he could be that he was alone, did he relax.

The chilli-red sand under the overhang was bone dry, yet outside a couple of inches of muddy-coloured ice covered the valley. Jarell shivered and slumped against a crumbling wall.

The stones behind him grew warm. As their heat passed through his body, every ache and bruise healed. Jarrel recognized the power.

"*Kundi!*" he said in surprise.

Welcome home, Jarell, the deep voice of his ancestor filled his head. *When you face your greatest test, all of Ulfrika will be watching.*

No pressure then, thought Jarell. *But I won't let you or Ulfrika down.*

You hold our future and our past in your hands. Remember that. The voice of Kundi's spirit faded into the emptiness of the cave.

Outside, a mechanical hum rose over the sound of rain. It was getting louder.

Jarell edged forward to take a peek. The hail had stopped but a storm still raged. He searched the sky for the strange whining sound.

Back from the direction he had come, he spotted a sleek black shape recklessly carving its way through the lightning and fierce winds.

As the craft dipped and dived, Jarell recognized its hawk-like wings. It belonged to Ayana's guards. During his first adventure in Ulfrika, he and Kimisi had "borrowed" – and crashed – one. They were powerful machines, but Jarell knew from experience they weren't designed to fly in a storm.

The pilot is a fool, Jarell thought. *They should land before—*

A jagged bolt of lightning hit the craft, and black material exploded from it like feathers. The hawk was still flying, but it had a deep orange gash in its side. The steady hum of its engines had become a stuttering whine.

Without warning, the craft dropped and plunged towards one of the high sandstone stacks. "No!" Jarell yelled, even though he knew the pilot couldn't hear him. "Steer away from the rocks!"

The hawk swerved just in time. A wing clipped the top of a stack, sending stones tumbling down. Then, with a burst of flames, its engines died completely.

"*Eject!*" Jarell shouted, his heart thumping through his chest. "*Eject now!*"

CHAPTER THREE

SANDSKIMMERS

Bang!

The hawk slammed into the valley floor. Thick smoke poured from its wings.

Jarell dashed from the overhang. He had to battle against the heavy wind and rain, but it didn't matter – he had to help the pilot escape before the craft exploded.

Reaching the back of the craft, Jarell slammed a green circle to open the door. Circuits whirred angrily under the panel before dying in a burst of sparks. *That's not good.*

He picked up the sharpest rock he could find and smashed it against the panel. Its metal edge crumpled and Jarell yanked the panel open. He saw a loose green wire among the rainbow of charred wires and plugged it back in.

The panel sparked and the door opened with a soft creak.

"Hello?" Jarell stepped inside. Broken glass crunched underfoot. Wires dangled overhead like jungle vines. He could smell burning, but thankfully the worst of the smoke remained outside. He ducked under a broken support beam.

As Jarell crept through the wreckage, the hairs on the back of his neck prickled. *Ayana's guards knew hawks couldn't cope with storms. Could one of Ikala's followers have stolen it?*

Jarell rushed to the cockpit. The empty pilot's chair was slowly turning like something out of a horror movie. Wisps of white smoke and a hissing sound seeped out of the edges of a broken panel hanging from the ceiling. Jarell swallowed and tiptoed around it.

A uniformed figure was using a power gauntlet to spray foam at a burning control panel. "Hey!" Jarell shouted. "Get out of here before this thing goes up!"

The pilot turned sharply, a reflective mask covering their face.

"Scared of a little fire, Jarell?!" a familiar voice asked. The figure tapped the mask with a finger and it retracted. Kimisi grinned at Jarell. "It's good to see you!"

"You too," Jarell said. "But this hawk is not going to fly again; it's going to explode! We need to get out of here."

Kimisi's eyes widened just a little. "It's not the worst idea you've had, Jarell," she said. They hurried out of the cockpit towards the exit, but Kimisi slowed to grab some things. "We need the crate with the orange stripe as well," she cried.

Jarell knew there was no point trying to get Kimisi to change her mind. He tried to lift the crate, but it was heavy. As he dragged it, broken glass screeched underneath.

"We need to take cover in case the craft blows," Jarell said as they jumped from the hawk. Through the billowing smoke, he spotted a mound nearby. "Over there, quick!"

"We need to take the crate!" Kimisi replied, dropping everything else in her arms.

Even with the two of them carrying the bulky box, it was hard work hauling it through the rain. *Come on*, Jarell silently urged. *We need to go faster.*

They had barely got behind the mound, when ... *boom!*

The craft exploded. Bits of burning wreckage rained down everywhere.

"Why do the hawks only crash when you're around, eh?" Kimisi laughed.

Jarell shook his head. It was good to be back with his friend.

The storm vanished as suddenly as it had appeared, the blanket of hailstones quickly melting to slush in the bright and cloudless sky. *Strange weather.*

"What are the odds of us meeting like this?" Jarell asked. "Do you think Ayana summoned the storm to bring us together?"

Kimisi glared at him. "That would indicate that Ancients think about us *mere* mortals, Jarell. I'm not so convinced."

Jarell blinked. Normally Kimisi had nothing but respect for Ancients, except Legsy, of course. "Has Ayana done something to upset you?" he asked.

Kimisi gave Jarell a long, cold stare. He guessed Ayana still hadn't risen from the waters of her ruined temple. Kimisi probably felt abandoned. Anyway, blowing Kimisi's hawk from the sky didn't sound like Ayana's style. *But if it wasn't her, who could it have been?*

"Enough talk of Ancients, eh," Kimisi said, changing the subject. "We have to—"

"Go to Fekuk and fight for the Iron Eagle," Jarell interrupted, pleased that he knew as much as Kimisi for once. "Legsy said Oufula and Ayana were married. Perhaps Oufula will change his mind if we remind him of the love and honour—"

Kimisi gave a mocking laugh. "The God of Thunder lacks honour, Jarell. He is self-centred and proud, not to mention flashy."

"Flashy?" Jarell was confused. "Like, with cars and jewels?"

Kimisi palmed her forehead. "No, *actually* flashy. His toys are flames and lightning. Playthings for a spoilt child. He finds it entertaining."

Jarell stared at what was left of the hawk. "How are we going to get to Oufula's city then? Can we cloudport?"

Kimisi shook her head but a broad grin split her face. With a wave of her gauntlet, the lid of the large rescued crate slid open.

"First, let me return this," she said, handing over the Staff of Kundi.

With a flick of his wrist, Jarell extended the staff to its full size. Three Iron Animals sprung to life as if waking from a deep sleep. The Iron Snake shone with a reddish-brown light. The Iron Crocodile's jade-green eyes blinked as it snapped it jaws. And the Iron Leopard narrowed its burning ember-red eyes. Jarell silently thanked them for waiting. He shrunk the staff again and hung it on his belt.

Kimisi then pulled out what looked like two slate-grey drain covers. Their surfaces glistened with fine gold circuits and a coal-black band around the edges. She threw them into the air. They expanded to the size of surfboards before floating at waist height. "Sandskimmers," she said proudly. "I assume you don't have these where you come from?"

"Only in movies," Jarell explained. "We call them hoverboards."

"What is the point of just hovering?" Kimisi asked. "These are better. Sandskimmers will take us to Fekuk fast, and stop us from getting eaten."

"Eaten?" Jarell gulped.

"Hungry creatures hide beneath the sand," Kimisi said as she pulled a sandskimmer close. "Let me show you how to ride. Oufula won't wait for us so I can't have you making us late."

Always late, Jarell thought. With a helping hand from Kimisi, he climbed on to the strange floating device and tried to balance. It swayed like it wanted to throw him off.

"Your legs tell the sandskimmer where to go," Kimisi said. "Think of it like a conversation."

How hard can it be? Jarell thought. He bent his knees as if he was on a surfboard and leaned forward. The sandskimmer shot out from under his legs, throwing him to the ground.

Jarell scrambled up before Kimisi could offer him a hand. He could feel his face burning with embarrassment.

"Even lemon-tailed chimps learn to balance before they can climb, Jarell. Let me show you." Kimisi boarded her own sandskimmer and set off slowly. "Try again."

He studied what Kimisi was doing. Rather than a surfing pose, Kimisi used an Ingalo-like stance.

Back on the sandskimmer, Jarell did the same and felt better connected with the sway of the board. Instead of leaning forward, he simply shifted his weight on to his front foot. The sandskimmer responded gently and smoothly. It picked up speed and Jarell swept it out in a large circle around his friend.

"*Haba*, you've got it!" Kimisi cheered.

Bringing his weight back to the middle, Jarell slowed the board to a stop. "You lead, I'll follow," he said, planning to take it slowly.

With a nod, Kimisi shot off.

Jarell couldn't even think about it; he had to keep up. Off he flew, weaving around the boulders and prickly bushes in his path. He steadied himself as the odd low mound caused the sandskimmer to launch into the air. As the rocky landscape gave way to a stretch of flat sand, Jarell felt confident enough to go for it.

He rushed forward with the wind in his face and let out a whoop of delight. *Lucas, eat your heart out*, Jarell thought.

Suddenly, Kimisi swerved off to the side. She

waved her arms at him and pointed to a rippling patch of sand. "Watch out!" she shouted, but Jarell was going too fast to change course without falling off.

As the sandskimmer neared, two huge pincers burst out of the writhing sand. They were followed by the rest of the enormous, striped, armoured body of a scorpion. Jarell ducked as its pincers snapped at him, but the sandskimmer wobbled and started to slow.

The scorpion leapt forward again. This time, aiming the pulsing stinger of its long emerald tail at him.

Regaining his balance, Jarell swerved the sandskimmer. The stinger smashed into the ground and the scorpion lunged with its claws once more.

"Outrun it!" Kimisi screamed.

Jarell leaned forward, racing the sandskimmer

faster than he had dared! But the scorpion was fast. One mistake and he knew either its pincers or its poisonous tail would get him. Jarrel scanned the landscape for a way to escape, but there was nothing but sand. "This way!" Kimisi yelled, swerving towards the cliffs.

He shot after her. The scorpion followed.

He hurtled towards the solid wall of the cliffs as they loomed larger and larger. *What's the plan?* he wondered, then suddenly Kimisi disappeared into the cliff face.

Jarell kicked out, twisting the sandskimmer after her. Then he spotted it. A cave!

Plunging into the darkness, the headlights of

the sandskimmer blazed on. They caught every jagged edge coming towards him. Behind, the scorpion kept following, the patterns on its skin glowing rave red and sick-bay green as it squeezed easily through the tunnel.

"Lie down!" Kimisi shouted from somewhere ahead of him.

Jarell threw himself down on the board. The sudden shift of weight propelled it even faster, shooting the sandskimmer through the narrowest gaps between the boulders.

Seconds later, both Jarell and Kimisi sailed out into bright sunshine – the scorpion trapped behind them.

As they slowed to catch their breath, Kimisi pointed out the claw marks on the back of his sandskimmer. "Baku!" Kimisi shook her head. "Why didn't you fly around the nest?"

Jarell swallowed hard. "Let me guess – that was a giant desert scorpion?"

"You're lucky," Kimisi said. "Kundi nearly lost a whole army to them once. Those scorpions are loyal to Ikala."

Kimisi told him the story of Kundi and the scorpions as they set off again. Jarell tried to listen but his heartbeat was still loud in his ears. He hoped he'd never meet a giant scorpion again.

In the distance, he spotted an old man trekking awkwardly through the sand.

"Kimisi!" Jarell called out, swerving towards the figure. "That old man is just asking to be eaten! We have to help!"

"Wait, Jarell!" Kimisi flew closer. "No one comes here without a reason. What if it's Ikala in disguise?"

"What if it isn't?" Jarell answered. "Kundi

wouldn't leave a helpless old man in danger."

But still, he slowed as he approached the stranger. The man's clothes were ill-fitting and tattered, as if he had thrown on the first discarded robes he'd found. His skin looked dry, like baked clay, and his ash-coloured hair and sunken eyes added to his worn and ancient appearance.

Jarell stopped a scorpion's length away from him. The old man looked up. "Mbata," he greeted with a kind smile. He leaned delicately on a rough staff. "I'm Tomi."

"Mbata, I'm Jarell," Jarell replied, aware of his friend keeping her distance. "And that is Kimisi."

"Mbata, Kimisi," Tomi called with a feeble

wave. "What are you doing here? Don't you know the dangers? Aren't you scared?"

Jarell went to speak, but Kimisi cut him off. "We're just passing," she said, coming closer. "We want to see the fabled city of Fekuk."

Tomi looked to the heavens. "*Ah*, the city that floats in the sky. I never thought I would get to gaze upon its wonders again."

"Jarell," Kimisi said with a cough. "Can I speak with you?"

Jarell skimmed after Kimisi until they were just out of Tomi's earshot. "Let me guess," he said. "Something about him doesn't seem right – but didn't you say the same thing about me when we first met?"

Kimisi opened her mouth to respond. Then she crossed her arms. "Not the same," she finally said.

But seeing that he'd won the argument, Jarell

returned to Tomi. "Why don't you ride on my sandskimmer to Fekuk, Tomi. It'll be faster and safer than being on foot."

"Could my travelling companion come too?" Tomi said. "He's run off ahead to find the best path as I don't move as fast as him. I'm sure his legs are tired, though."

A companion? Doubt began to form in Jarell's mind. If Tomi wasn't travelling alone, was he really as harmless as he looked?

CHAPTER FOUR

THE FLOATING CITY

Kimisi brought her sandskimmer closer. "Jarell,"
she hissed. "Let's go before this companion turns
up. Tomi might not even know if Ikala's tricked
him."

Jarell bit his lip. He definitely didn't like waiting.
Maybe Kimisi has a point.

"Auntie Kimisi!" a high-pitched voice called

as its owner climbed over a sand dune. Jarell grinned. He instantly recognized Bo-de's cheeky smile. A distant relation of Kimisi, his family lived near Sila, the City of Clay, so what was he doing here?

"Bo-de?" Kimisi gasped. She cruised towards him. Bo-de's smile quickly disappeared as she hauled him on to the skimmer. "Baku! Why are you so far from home and alone?" she asked in a stern voice that made even Jarell shudder.

"We met on the road," Tomi began. "He said he would—"

"Silence!" Kimisi snapped. She turned to Bo-de. "Your mother will be worried sick!"

"Can you not cloudport him home?" Jarell suggested. Bo-de pouted; he hated missing out on adventures.

Kimisi huffed. "My cloudporting device has

been malfunctioning lately. I'm sure it's down to Ikala. He makes everything worse." She turned to Tomi and snapped, "What were you thinking bringing a child *here*?"

Tomi raised his hands defensively. "We met far from his homelands, Kimisi. I thought the child would be safer with me than wandering alone."

At that, Jarell looked at Kimisi and shrugged. If there was one thing their adventures had taught them, they were always better off together.

Kimisi flared her nostrils. "Bo-de, you will ride with me in silence. Do you understand?"

Bo-de nodded solemnly but, as Kimisi looked away, Jarell saw a massive grin appear on his face. It was funny to think that this Bo-de knew nothing of the beetle-spider that had shapeshifted into him during Jarell's last adventure. Jarell was glad Bo-de didn't know.

"Let's not waste more time," Kimisi said, interrupting Jarell's thoughts.

Her sandskimmer soared off, leaving Jarell to help the old man climb aboard his own. For someone so thin and fragile looking, Tomi weighed more than he expected.

"Umm, I haven't driven any passengers before," Jarell said nervously. "You might—"

Tomi waved his explanation away and sat down cross-legged on the sandskimmer. "I'm not worried, but your friend is getting away," he said softly.

Jarell saw Kimisi getting smaller and smaller in the distance and set off. The sandskimmer definitely struggled with the extra weight, threatening to throw them off at every turn. But Tomi sat silently, unfazed by the rough ride.

After a while Kimisi slowed, letting Jarell catch

up. They moved through another valley before coming to a huge slope covered in mist.

On the other side, they found themselves on the edge of a humongous volcanic crater. High above their heads floated the city in the sky: Fekuk.

Jarell recognized this hovering city. He'd drawn it. From its centre, massive, angular buildings cut out in every direction like the points on a star – each far bigger than any skyscraper Jarell had seen on Earth. The geometric spikes gleamed with platinum silvers, deep azure blues and rich bright purples. Sparks of electricity cascaded over the huge, spiked ball, weaving between buildings that seemed to be built on top of other buildings.

They slid off the sandskimmers to take in the view.

"By the Ancients— I can't believe— It's wonderful—" Bo-de gabbled so fast it was a wonder he could breathe. *So much for not speaking a word*, Jarell laughed to himself.

"Fekuk," whispered Tomi.

"How are we getting up there?" Jarell asked.

"I don't know." Kimisi looked stumped. "I was planning to fly there with my craft, but—"

"It crashed after being struck by a bolt of lightning," Tomi interrupted.

Kimisi whirled around to face him. "How could you have known that?" she demanded, reaching for her spear. "Unless the lightning had something to do with you."

Jarell caught Kimisi's arm to stop her, but Tomi laughed. "Would I walk if I had any special powers? No. However, Oufula never changes."

Kimisi relaxed her arm and Jarell let go. "It makes sense," he said. "Oufula is the God of Thunder. He could have caused the storm."

Tomi hobbled forward. "I'll help you get into the floating city." The old man dug into the folds of his cloak. He pulled out a small carved pipe wrapped with cords and strung with cowrie shells. "This will get someone's attention." It clinked lightly as he held it up. Its dark wood reminded Jarell of Legsy's mirror back in Fades.

"A marsa flute?" Kimisi whispered in awe. "So rare."

"Let me try," pleaded Bo-de, trying to grab it.

Tomi held it out of reach. "Someone with stronger lungs, perhaps. How about you, Jarell?"

Taking the flute, Jarell held it to his lips. While each separate part of the pipe seemed fragile, together they radiated power. He took a deep breath and blew.

A note like the sweetest birdsong flew from the pipe. It danced around them, rising and falling and getting louder rather than fading. Omari's sound system was tame by comparison.

Jarell took another breath. "That's enough," Tomi said, taking the pipe back. He pointed towards the round aircraft speeding towards them. "Our chariot awaits."

What floated towards them had an almost see-through shell shaped like an orb; it radiated a rainbow of colours just like a giant soap bubble. It landed with a gentle bounce before a doorway slid open and a mechanical soldier marched out.

"Is that a ... *robot*?" Jarell whispered.

"We stand in the land of the ancient-future," Tomi said. "It's amazing what can be fashioned with a bit of ingenuity."

"State your business," demanded the soldier.

Tomi stood up straight. "To compete for the Iron Eagle."

"What?" both Jarell and Kimisi said at once.

Tomi looked at their shocked faces and shrugged. "You never asked."

"I wish to fight for the prize too," Kimisi told the guard.

"And me," Jarell added.

"I wish to—" Bo-de said, stepping forward. Before he could say anything else, Kimisi covered his mouth.

"He is too young to compete," she said. "He wishes for passage to the city as my supporter. The rules permit one each, do they not?"

The robot beeped. "The young human can attend as your guest."

Bo-de pulled away from Kimisi. He looked furious at not being able to participate.

"Follow." The soldier led them into the craft. A floor-to-ceiling window that gave close to a 360-degree view was pretty much all that was inside, except a tiny royal-blue console the soldier plugged itself into. As the doors closed, the aircraft lifted smoothly into the sky.

Gazing down, it was much easier to get a sense of the vastness of the crater now, and then Jarell was looking at the valleys stretching out in every direction, and then up at the star shaped city they were heading towards.

"Prepare for turbulence," the soldier announced.

Turbulence? Something invisible slammed through Jarell's body. It shook him like jelly, then vanished. By the looks on their faces, Kimisi, Tomi and Bo-de had all experienced the same thing. "Fekuk's force field," Tomi explained. "It's transparent and protects the city from intruders."

Oufula really does like to keep his city private, Jarell thought.

The craft zipped along one of the giant spikes. Jarell could see the intricately carved Ulfrikan symbols that covered every building. Long vines with exotic flowers were hung on star-shaped balconies. More flowering plants weaved their way along the bridges between buildings. Everywhere people in long flowing robes went about their business.

"People actually *live* here?" Bo-de said, mouth

wide. "You think Oufula allows any travellers to stay?"

Jarell was about to answer when the ship fell into shadow, entering a tunnel that led them through buildings deep into the city.

Moments later, the craft landed in the middle of a stadium that dwarfed the biggest sports arenas back home. Even a cup final would be lost in it.

"Leave, now," the soldier commanded, opening the door.

Flags snapped in the wind above the vast stadium. Beneath them, the spectators' stands were packed. It felt like the whole city was here. Their chants and cheers made the hairs on Jarell's arms prickle. Everyone was dressed in long, brightly patterned robes. Some had painted faces, some blew whistles or banged drums. Jarell could imagine his brother enjoying this crowd.

Staring down at the arena floor from the doorway, it looked like they were going to step into thin air. It had to be more than a mirror-smooth surface, Jarell realized. For despite the reflection of sharp blue sky dotted with tiny white puffs of cloud, none of the buildings that surrounded them appeared.

When Jarell stepped on it, the ground crunched underfoot. It was made of tiny white grains arranged in patterns that reminded him of lilies.

Bo-de scooped up a handful of white flakes and tried to put them in his pocket, but Kimisi made him return them.

"What is this?" Jarell said, rubbing the grains between his fingers. They flickered with a fire of pure white light somewhere deep inside. They were mesmerizing.

"Sky salt," said Tomi. "It has magic qualities, like reflection and transformation. But do not be fooled by its illusions."

Jarell looked back, but the ship had already gone. Behind them, in the centre of the main stand, separate from the crowd, was a throne made of glass thunderbolts.

A soldier marched over and led Bo-de away. After his protests fell on deaf ears, Bo-de called back, "Good luck! You're going to need it."

Tomi frowned. "The child is upset."

Kimisi shrugged. "He'll get over it. We don't need the distraction."

"Would I count as a distraction?" a voice from Jarell's nightmares rumbled behind him.

Jarell spun around to face Ikala. He had never met the evil sorcerer in person. A dangerous smile played on Ikala's lips, but his stare was one

of pure hatred. Under a flowing blood-red cloak, the sorcerer's armour bristled with spikes. Electric flame-red pulses flickered over the same metal gauntlets Ikala had used in his battle against Ayana.

"Nothing to say after getting in my way so often?" Ikala tutted, and ran his tongue across his teeth. "Surely I am owed an apology." He shook his head. "Luck saved you from the Were-hyenas, Zin and the Asanbosam. That *luck* ends now."

"How dare you speak of luck to Jarell. He is the heir of Kundi. Our Future Hero." Kimisi growled, stepping forward with her spear at full length.

"*Kundi?*" Ikala laughed. "Future Hero?" He clenched his gauntlets into fists and they started to charge with energy. "You look a bit like him, Jarell, but you're weak. Will you scream in pain the same way he did, if I were to attack?"

Jarell unfroze, slipping the Staff of Kundi from his belt and extending it. "Try me!"

"You'll lose, Jarell. You are a loser just like your pathetic ancestor!" Ikala spat.

"The way I hear it went, *you* were the one who lost, not Kundi," Jarell snapped, getting ready to strike first.

A cool hand gently touched Jarell's wrist. Tomi was holding him and Kimisi. "Stand down, my friends. Fighting before the contest is against the rules," he said calmly. His words had a power of their own.

Jarell shrunk his weapon and stepped back. Tomi was right. Even Kimisi had lowered her spear.

"You look like a pauper, yet you speak like a

king," Ikala said, staring at Tomi. "Don't I know you from somewhere?"

Tomi ignored Ikala, and turned back to Jarell. "It is disrespectful to the God of Thunder to attack another competitor without permission. Oufula would be displeased."

"I would," a voice boomed around them as a bolt of lightning smashed into the ground and sprayed them with sky salt.

Between them now stood a giant with arms like tree trunks. The scarlet material around the Ancient's waist crackled with electricity. A crown of flames sprouted on his head, then surged down his neck, snaking along his arms. Once the fire reached the God of Thunder's hands, the flames gathered, forming two massive battle axes.

Jarell blinked. *Kimisi was right about him being flashy.*

"Fighting is reserved for the games!" Oufula roared with laughter. "And I look forward to the entertainment."

He clanged the fiery battle axes over his head. The arena rocked with thunder. Oufula's axes exploded into flames and in their place, a copper-bronze bird appeared. It screeched and swooped around the god with wings longer than Jarell's arms and talons as sharp as daggers. It landed on Oufula's shoulder.

Oufula held out his hands and silenced everyone watching in the stands. "People of Fekuk!" the god called. "Our twelve competitors are here!"

The crowd roared. The battle for the Iron Eagle had commenced.

CHAPTER FIVE

A SACRIFICE IS DEMANDED

All twelve of the competitors stood in a semicircle in front of Oufula and his glass throne. Each contestant looked dangerous in their own way, Jarell decided. One woman even had long braids that ended in sharp crystal shards.

Above them, Oufula sat proudly in his seat. His back as straight as a blade. Around the stadium, spectators drummed their fists against their chests and roared. Flares poured sickly yellow smoke across the crowd.

Jarell caught sight of Bo-de sat in the section behind the Ancient, flanked on either side by robot guards. It looked like he was trying to hide something up his sleeve, but still he gave Jarell a wave.

Oufula cleared his throat. The stadium grew silent again. "If any contestant wishes to leave, step forward now and speak."

Jarell drew a deep breath and stepped forward. A murmur electrified the crowd.

"The descendant of Kundi wishes to *quit*?" Oufula asked, his face shocked.

Jarell paused. "No, Oufula, I am not quitting. I want to give you the chance to reconsider holding this tournament. The Iron Eagle doesn't belong in Ikala's hands, and if he wins it, Ulfrika will be in danger. Please listen to reason—"

Kimisi pulled at his arm. "Forgive Jarell, Oufula. He does not know—"

"Silence!" Oufula spoke, and there was thunder behind his voice. "What gives you the right to demand anything of me, mortal? What will be, will be! Who's to say where the Iron Eagle belongs? Perhaps I should keep it for myself. Maybe even take the other Iron Animals' powers for my own too."

Jarell gulped, unsure of the Ancient's seriousness. Even the evil sorcerer Ikala seemed uncertain.

Oufula let out a deep laugh. "Do not worry, kin of Kundi. I am a god of the Sky, trinkets from the land are of no interest to me. I simply seek merriment. Excitement—"

"This tournament is just *entertainment* for you?" Jarell asked.

"Exactly," Oufula stated. "And recently, boredom here has become rampant. A good ruler provides his people with what they crave! Now, enough. Pay your entrance fees!"

Huh? Jarell thought, turning to Kimisi, but even she looked confused.

"Surely a griot knows that every true prize comes with a sacrifice," Tomi whispered. "That's the way stories go. To gain the Iron Eagle, something of equal or greater value must be risked."

"Something of greater value?" Jarell echoed. "Like what?"

"Like this!" Ikala shouted over the sound of metal scraping against the salt.

Five Were-hyenas, ruthless beasts Jarell had encountered on his first trip to Ulfrika, dragged a large midnight-black chest across the arena. Upright on two legs, their panting breaths sounded like cackles, and dirty tongues stuck out between their needle-sharp teeth.

The chest was covered in spikes with scarlet-red symbols gashed into the top. The Were-hyenas stopped in front of Oufula, then scarpered – leaving the chest behind. Ikala stepped forward proudly. "The second greatest weapon I possess!" he declared. With a click, the chest sprung open towards Oufula. From where he stood, Jarell couldn't see what was inside no matter how hard he strained.

Oufula seemed disappointed. "Only the second? Any competition of mine demands you risk your most coveted asset."

Ikala paused. "The first is my own intelligence, God of Thunder. And I do not intend to hand over my brain."

"Very well." Oufula nodded. Jarell noticed the Ancient's disappointment seemed to transform into respect. "The next contestant, come forward!"

The next contestant to offer up their fee was Tomi. The old man walked forward gingerly and moved to climb the glass steps of the throne. Mechanical guards blocked his way.

"What I pledge is private, Oufula," Tomi said. "And worth more because of it."

Oufula considered. "Let him pass."

The robots shifted out of the way. Tomi reached the foot of the throne and whispered something in the Ancient's ear. Jarell wished he knew what the old man was saying. Oufula's head jerked with surprise.

"Think carefully about that sacrifice, old man," Oufula said sincerely.

What could Tomi have promised, Jarell wondered, *to make Oufula hesitate?*

"I am sure," Tomi confirmed.

"Very well," Oufula said, waving Tomi away. "Who is next?"

Kimisi stepped forward, her hands shaking as she pulled the spear from her belt. "The Spear of Light, great Oufula." She placed the weapon respectfully on the floor and bowed. "It has been in my family for fourteen generations."

"No," Oufula scoffed. "This weapon may be valued in many stories, but it does not mean as much to *you* as you think. Try again."

Kimisi shot Jarell a worried look, bending down to retrieve her spear. "There is only one thing I value more: my griot powers."

Oufula's eyes came alive.

"Kimisi, you can't!" Jarell begged. "What if—"

"Too late," Oufula interrupted, waving Kimisi away. "Fee accepted, challenger."

Jarell swallowed as Oufula's attention swung to him. *What could I offer?* he pondered. *He couldn't pledge the Staff of Kundi. In the awful event that Ikala won the Iron Eagle, Jarell would need all the power the staff could muster to try to stop him.*

He thought back to Kimisi's offer. The God of Thunder had wanted her to give up something personal. *What do I have other than my ability to draw?*

He felt sick; drawing was everything to him. Without it, he might never have even found out about Ulfrika. But would it be worthy enough? He met Oufula's eyes, but just before he could speak, Ikala cut in.

"How can a runt, not even from the kingdom of Ulfrika, be considered for this contest?" the sorcerer spat. "This *Jarell* is a stranger to Ulfrikans. His family deserted their homeland generations ago to cross the universes. To explore other dimensions."

Oufula crossed his legs and chuckled. "I thought you were happy to see the back of Kundi's descendants, Ikala, all those years ago."

Ikala's eyes narrowed. Jarell assumed the sorcerer didn't get backchat very often.

"True," Ikala replied, "but the fact remains, Jarell is not Ulfrikan. Foreigners should not concern themselves with Ulfrikan affairs."

"I cannot say I disagree," Oufula said. Jarell's heart pounded as Oufula actually considered Ikala's harsh words. "Contestants must have walked on Ulfrikan soil and breathed in Ulfrikan air. They must be truly at home in Ulfrika."

Ulfrika is the one place I've always felt at home.

Jarell was shaking so badly with anger that he couldn't bring himself to speak.

Kimisi stepped forward, her hands curled into fists. "Jarell has the blood of Kundi. That makes him Ulfrikan!" She shot Ikala a withering stare, then turned to Oufula. "Jarell is fighting to save Ulfrika, while you ask for entertainment. If you give Ikala what he wants, you betray Ayana — worse, you betray Ulfrika!"

Oufula's throne rose in the air. Veins in his neck throbbed with displeasure. "You speak to me of betrayal? Ayana didn't ask before hiding the Iron Eagle in my city. Did she think to trick me into protecting it? She brought danger to Fekuk and made us a target. I am only trying to get rid of it for the sake of my people." The God of Thunder paused, then smirked. "Why not have some fun while doing so? Ikala makes a sound argument.

What do you say, heir of Kundi?" he asked, easing himself back on to his throne.

With a deep breath, Jarell forced his anger to settle. This time, he needed to out-think Ikala. "I can be many things at once. I am British. I am Jamaican. I am Ulfrikan as well, because that is where my ancestors are from!" He felt his voice rising and swallowed. "I have walked on Ulfrikan soil, breathed its air, been healed by its power." He glanced at Kimisi. "I have been welcomed as family."

"Your proclamations bore me," Oufula hissed. Before Jarell could protest, the Ancient turned to ask the remaining contestants for their offers which they gave with steady voices.

Sometimes yuh have to give up what yuh know to gain something more. Uncle Malcolm's words echoed in Jarell's mind. *My ability to go home,*

Jarell realized. Even the thought of never seeing his family again caused his chest to ache, but he had to risk everything to save Ulfrika.

"I offer my ability to return home to my family," Jarell blurted, a lump catching in his throat as the words left his mouth. The wing symbol pulsed on his head as Tomi grabbed him by the arm.

"Too much," the old man warned. "Trust me when I say, there is no pain worse than being cut off from the ones you love and the place you call home."

Jarell heard the regret in Tomi's voice, but

he didn't take his offer back. "I have made my decision," he said firmly.

"An offer has been made..." Oufula said. The crowd grew silent. "And accepted. A worthy sacrifice, Jarell. The greatest warriors must always be prepared to lose what they love most." Oufula turned to his spectators, encouraging their cheers and applause.

"In Fekuk, we respect greatness above all!" he bellowed as lightning blazed above him in the shape of an eagle. "The twelve hopefuls have paid their fees to face three challenges. Whoever is left standing by the end will be crowned the greatest warrior. Let the contest begin!"

CHAPTER SIX

AFIDI THE MIGHTY

Jarell stood across from the biggest man he had ever seen. The God of Thunder had announced him as Afidi the Mighty. His muscles looked like they had been carved from stone. Veins as thick as snakes flexed beneath his skin as the warrior stretched and warmed up for battle. Jarell clutched the staff hanging from his belt. No one else had their weapons out, but he couldn't see how he could defeat Afidi one-on-one without it.

The circular steel platform they stood on floated high above the arena with a faint mechanical hum. Thin lines etched into the platform's polished surface gave their bare feet something to grip. A ring of flashing amber lights marked the long drop to the hard sky-salt floor.

Jarell stole a quick glance across at the other platforms that had also risen into the air.

Kimisi's opponent paced the narrow edge of their platform like a jackal. The warrior's braids, which ended with spiky crystals, glinted menacingly. She growled at his friend, revealing sharpened teeth. Kimisi stared back with crossed arms as if deeply unimpressed.

Tomi's opponent couldn't have been more than a few years older than Jarell. With black hair coiled with thread and a sharp, chiselled face, the warrior held Tomi's gaze with a careful, calculated look. Jarell sensed he already knew exactly how to defeat the old man.

Jarell glanced at Ikala's match. Ultimately, it was the only one that really mattered. Ikala could not be allowed to win the tournament. The enchanter faced a skinny, nervous warrior who looked ready to jump rather than face the most evil sorcerer ever known to Ulfrika. *Not a fair match*, Jarell thought. Ikala yawned as if he had already lost interest in the battle to come.

Jarell turned his attention back to the giant Afidi, ready to make his first move with the staff. He had one chance to strike before the warrior would be across the small platform and on him.

"The first challenge is both a test of strength and agility!" Oufula announced. "The rules are simple.

Hand-to-hand combat. No weapons. Fall off the platform and into the anti-gravity force field before your opponent, and you are out of the games."

As Jarell let go of the staff on his belt, Oufula's words sank in. *Hand-to-hand combat.* A wicked grin appeared on Afidi's chiselled face. *How am I going to beat this guy without my staff?* Jarell wondered.

"Do not lose heart, Jarell!" Kimisi yelled from her platform. "We have faced fiercer foes and won."

"I wouldn't want to be in your shoes, Jarell!" Bo-de called cheerfully from the crowd below.

"Smile," Afidi said, beating his meaty fists against his chest. "To be defeated by Afidi the Mighty, Afidi the Stomper of Spirits, is an honour."

A roll of thunder crashed around the stadium. "Begin!" Oufula boomed.

Instantly the circular platform tilted violently and Jarell went tumbling headfirst. He clawed at the steel surface trying to save himself. He slid close to the platform's edge, towards nothing but clouds and thin air. *This can't be happening.*

Suddenly, the plinth moved again and his momentum slowed. Jarell scrambled back from the edge and got to his feet. He wasn't alone, nearly all the contestants had been taken by surprise, but everyone was still on their plinth.

The crowd screamed with excitement, loving every moment.

With a ferocious cry, Afidi sprinted towards him.

Don't make it easy, get further away from the edge, Jarell scolded himself. He sprung forward to meet Afidi's attack, but before they could clash the platform lurched yet again.

Jarell used the sudden movement to change direction and Afidi's fist brushed against the side of his head, just grazing the skin. Jarell slipped behind his opponent.

The platform stopped moving again. Afidi spun around with unexpected grace. "You bounce about like a pod from a suku tree, but I tire of this game," he spat.

Slipping into an Ingalo stance, Jarell got ready to defend himself. Afidi stalked forward, studying every move Jarell made.

A sudden scream from another platform made

them both turn. Jarell watched in horror as an unlucky contestant disappeared into the clouds below.

I really hope there is an anti-gravity force field down there, Jarell thought. *Maybe it would have been better to stay at Uncle Malcolm's party.*

A flicker in the corner of his eye caught Jarell's attention. Afidi sprung forward again, ready to attack as the platform see-sawed. The giant stumbled a little and froze, but Jarell could see that he was ever so slightly shaking.

He's absolutely terrified, Jarell realized. When the platform was still, Afidi moved nimbly like a cat, but when it rolled even a bit, the big lump went stiff, as if he had no control over his actions. Jarell let out a breath. As long as the platform moved, he was safe.

"Nicely done, sorcerer!" Oufula shouted. Jarell

stole a glance at the God of Thunder, cheering the loss of the skinny contestant. *I wonder if he cares who wins?*

Bowing, Ikala glanced across at Jarell. The sorcerer grinned even as his platform juddered to the left. Ikala certainly wasn't scared.

Jarell's platform stopped moving and Afidi rushed at him. Jarell dodged a high kick and slid under the giant. Then the metal surface tipped again.

Jarell glanced at the other platforms. Two on one side of him were already moving, but the next three only started to turn one after another. He glanced to make sure Afidi hadn't decided to suddenly risk moving, then checked back. There was a delay of a few seconds between each platform, but they all tilted in the same pattern. *Left, left, right, up, left.*

The two platforms on his left stopped moving and Jarell got ready. When their own plinth steadied, Afidi barrelled forward, trying desperately to land a punch. Jarell pitched himself under the giant's swinging arms and slid out behind him. Afidi spun around, but the platform had started the sequence again.

Jarell quickly counted the remaining contestants. Four pairs were left, but no one else seemed to have picked up on the sequence. *This was how he could beat Afidi.*

Jarell thought of his Ingalo lessons with Legsy. *Be fluid, let your body sway and become one with the platform.* "Be like a wave," Jarell muttered as the platform stilled yet again.

Afidi sniggered. "What are you talking about, twig?" He drew back open hands and shot forward before the platform rocked into motion again.

Jarell rode the platform like a sandskimmer, keeping his balance as it jerked. *Left, left, right, up, left.* Afidi stumbled. *An opening.* Jarell used the recoil of the platform and thrust forward, delivering a powerful kick to Afidi's back.

Afidi sprawled clumsily to the floor, turned to Jarell and growled like a feral dog as he got to his feet. The platform tilted again, and with even more force. *Be the wave.* Jarell used the motion of the platform once more and struck out at the giant's leg. Afidi tripped, landing flat on his belly.

"You little worm!" Afidi hissed, getting to his feet.

The platform was still for less than a second before it started the rolling sequence again. Jarell sprung forward and delivered a swift kick to Afidi's chest, sending him flailing towards the edge. The warrior desperately clawed at the steel, leaving deep scratches, and then he was out of sight.

Jarell thought he'd feel jubilant at winning, but somehow he just felt empty. Plus, Kimisi and Tomi were still in the heat of battle. He focused all his attention on Kimisi's contest against the warrior with the crystal-tipped braids and sharpened teeth. The warrior launched a frenzied attack at Kimisi, her arms and legs raining blows on his friend. *Come on, Kimisi, you've got this.*

Forced back from the middle of the platform, Kimisi parried the strikes using her wrists and elbows. She just managed to duck under the last of the blows, when the platform rocked again and she was thrown off balance. Her opponent delivered a roundhouse kick, catching Kimisi unexpectedly in the stomach. Kimisi's arms shot out, circling in the air to keep herself on her feet. Her mouth rounded into a perfect O of surprise.

She was in trouble.

Every muscle in Jarell's body tightened. *She's going to lose!* he thought.

The warrior lunged forward, but Kimisi dodged her with ease, tilting perfectly with the steel platform, and Jarell realized that she had been faking her distress. Kimisi sprung forward with a punch.

The warrior balanced on the edge of the platform, but her fight was over. With a delicate jab of the finger, Kimisi pushed her over the edge.

Jarell cheered. "You did it!"

Kimisi's grin quickly vanished. "Tomi!"

Jarell turned to the final match being played. Tomi was struggling to beat off a flurry of acrobatic kicks from the young warrior with the threaded hair. It was amazing Tomi had lasted so long.

How do I help? Jarell wondered. Was there a way he could tell Tomi about the pattern of movement with the platforms? *Perhaps I—*

His thoughts broke off as a massive hand landed on his shoulder and whipped him around.

CHAPTER SEVEN

THE MAGIC MAZE

Jarell found himself looking up at Afidi. "But … you … fell!" he stuttered.

"Only a fool tests the depth of a river with no feet," Afidi snarled.

"What does that even mean?" Jarell cried as Afidi dug his fingers into Jarell's collar and lifted him into the air. Afidi just laughed and carried Jarell

to the edge of the platform. Jarell tried twisting
and wriggling to get free, but Afidi's grip was
like iron.

If the giant threw him off the platform, that was
it. He was out of the competition and banished
from returning home to his family.

"Did you think *you* were special?" Afidi yelled.
"Did you really think you could beat me?"

Jarell felt dizzy as he peered down
into the clouds. *Think, Jarell,*

think! he urged himself. *What can you see? What can you use?*

Afidi's head was shaved, but his tree trunk of a neck was covered in thick leather armour. *That'll have to do*, Jarell decided. As the giant leaned back to throw him, Jarell grabbed hold of the armour. He twisted his fingers beneath the leather strapping.

Afidi laughed as he went to toss Jarell off the platform, but soon cursed in frustration as he found Jarell securely latched to him.

"Release me, worm!" Afidi roared.

"You first!" Jarell hissed.

The platform tilted again. Afidi grunted as he shifted back to the centre, his hands loosening their grip for just a second. *Now's my chance!* Jarell forced himself from the giant's arms and used his mountainous body as a climbing frame. He landed on the rocking platform knowing exactly which way the plinth would move next.

He crooked a finger and beckoned the giant insolently. As the giant lashed out, Jarell jumped out of the way and the platform juddered again. Afidi lost his balance. Before he could steady himself, Jarell shouldered Afidi as hard as he could in the belly.

Like an oak, Afidi fell. The high-tech platform shuddered under his weight, but it kept moving. The giant started to slide. As his legs went over the edge, Afidi flipped over and dug his fingers into the steel surface.

A screeching noise ripped through Jarell's ears as deep ruts appeared under the giant's nails. Artificially long and strong iron-sharp nails that dug deeper and deeper in the surface.

Afidi was left hanging with just his arms on the

platform. *So that's how he survived the first time! That's cheating!*

Jarell lifted his foot to stamp on Afidi's hands, but hesitated. *It was something Ikala would do.* His ancestor Kundi would never have won that way.

Instead, Jarell edged closer to the giant and crouched down.

"Concede, Afidi. I will try and persuade Oufula to give back whatever you offered him," he said. "I don't want to win like this."

The giant muttered something, straining as he dangled over the edge.

"I don't understand," Jarell spoke, leaning in closer. Suddenly, he was filled with that tingle he got when he knew trouble was heading his way. Jarell clocked the sinews pulsing in the giant's shoulders getting ready to do something.

As fast as a cobra, the warrior tried to grab

Jarell, but Jarell pulled away faster. The giant's gamble had failed. Afidi hung in the air for a second.

"Well played, *twig*," Afidi spat, before tumbling into the clouds below.

Jarell collapsed back on the steel platform, his energy drained. He looked around and realized that his had been the last match to finish. Tomi had survived his battle as well. The old man and Kimisi looked at him and pressed their fists against their chests. Jarell returned the gesture as the platforms slowly floated back down to the sky-salt floor.

The crowd's roar was deafening. Bo-de waved at him, trying to get closer, but the robot guards had him penned in.

Jarell stepped from the platform to the crunch of the white sparkling floor. Ikala scowled at him.

"Not bad," Oufula called from his throne.

The crowd hushed. "And then there were six. The display of strength and agility has been settled. Time for the second challenge!"

From around the stadium, thousands of people started to beat their drums. The pounding grew faster and more ominous as Oufula's mechanical soldiers herded the six remaining contestants to one end of the arena.

As they walked, Jarell noticed Kimisi wincing. "Are you hurt?"

"Baku, you can't get rid of me that easy," she replied, then laughed.

"We'll see about that," Ikala called back to them. "You and the runt barely survived that last challenge. I expected so much more from the fabled Future Hero."

Jarell felt his cheeks grow hot. He turned to Ikala, but Tomi caught his arm. "Focus on what matters," he whispered as if they had known each other for ages. "Don't let him get in your head."

When the remaining contestants were in place, three glistening crystal silver boxes rose on slender pillars at the far end of the arena. Each box opened to reveal an axe.

"To touch an axe of Fekuk is an honour," Oufula said, puffing out his chest. "The challenge is simple: get to an axe first and you will make it to the final round."

"So it's just a race?" Jarell asked.

Kimisi almost jumped with joy. "Haba, this is going to be easy! I'm the fastest runner in Ayana's guard."

"I wouldn't be so sure about the ease of this task," Tomi warned.

A cold wind gusted across the stadium. The sun dimmed, the sky-salt floor mirroring the dark, shadowy clouds that filled the sky. Oufula laughed as a roll of thunder clashed around them. Lightning erupted like strobe lights in a haunted house at a fun fair.

"It is a race, but also a test of cunning!" Oufula announced, before making a point of looking at Ikala and then Tomi. "No magic. If you use it, you will lose."

Jarell dreaded finding out what Oufula had planned. The Ancient liked throwing in surprises. He stared down at the floor trying not to panic. The sky-salt circles flickered, reflecting different colours as more lightning flashed overhead. Searing reds, violent oranges and toxic yellows. They reminded him of his journey to Fire Mountain, on his first trip to Ulfrika, and the first time he'd heard his ancestor's words in his head when he'd touched Ulfrikan soil. He couldn't give up.

"Cunning," Jarell repeated, thinking out loud. He turned to Kimisi. "Perhaps we could work together. It would help our chances."

Kimisi nodded. "Two heads are—" she started.

But before she could finish, Kimisi disappeared into a swirling grey cloud. Then it was Jarell's turn. A tornado whipped around him, stealing all the air from his lungs, and lifted him into the air. *Looks like cloudporting is not a problem for the God of Thunder*, Jarell realized, as his world became jumbled and dizzying. He landed with a thump, far from where he had been standing.

He saw Kimisi away to his right. She stood alone too. Jarell shot her a disappointed look. They always worked best when they were together. It was like Oufula had known their plan.

From his left, Jarell could sense Ikala's unflinching stare. A knot formed in his throat. The evil sorcerer would never give up on ruling Ulfrika. Only by reuniting the Staff of Kundi with all four of its Iron Animals would Jarell have any chance of stopping him.

A flash of light flooded the arena in front of him, forcing Jarell to shield his eyes. Peeking between his fingers, he could now see two blindingly bright walls of lightning blocking his view of the other contestants. The sleeve of his suit vibrated and he looked down. A small compartment had opened to reveal a pair of translucent yet iridescent wraparound shades. *Cool.* Putting them on, Jarell could look more carefully at the walls of electricity.

"Welcome to my maze of lightning!" Oufula's voice boomed around the arena, but Jarell couldn't see the stadium or prizes any more. "You see, a test of ingenuity! Will you let the maze defeat you, or will you come out on top? Will you come out at all?"

In the air in front of him, a flickering holographic symbol appeared. It changed shape. It changed again. *Wait*, he realized. *It's a countdown. That's got to be the symbol for seven. Six. Five.*

The wall behind the hologram vanished. Jarell was staring down a long corridor. The walls seethed with an angry electric crackle.

Two.

Jarell pictured the axes and their positions.

One.

The crowd cheered with excitement. Jarell sprinted into the maze. It wasn't going to be easy. Whenever he strayed off the dead centre of the path, painful sparks of electricity leapt at him. They stung like wasps.

He reached the first junction. *Left or right to*

the axes? Both directions looked the same, with more towering walls of lightning. He glanced back the way he had come, but the corridor behind him was collapsing in on itself creating a tidal wave of fire. He needed to decide fast.

Jarell sprinted left. Then the maze snaked right and Jarell reached a dead end. *Was going back and trying the other direction even still an option?*

As he took a few tentative steps back through the maze, another opening appeared. He dived into the new corridor without question.

Crack! Something exploded and knocked Jarell to the ground. Wisps of smoke danced in the air, forming shapes of axes and swords. *Magic*, he realized. *Another of Oufula's traps perhaps?*

Ears ringing, Jarell forced himself up. It was getting hotter. His high-tech suit was struggling to keep him cool. He stumbled on.

At the next junction, Jarell turned right. Then took another left. It was hard to think straight. His head was beginning to hurt from the light and constant buzzing.

The path ahead shimmered like heat rising in the desert. Jarell hesitated. *Was he losing it?* The corridor suddenly exploded into a massive fireball.

Jarell threw himself against the salt-covered floor. The flames rolled over his back, and his suit stopped it from burning him, but only just.

He got up. Fire now blocked the way. He

started coughing as black smoke filled the corridor. *Think*, Jarell urged himself. What had the fire brigade told them when they had visited school? Smoke is more dangerous than fire. *And smoke rises!* If you stay low where the air is cleaner, you have a better chance to escape.

Jarell flattened himself against the floor. Unlike the lightning, Jarell could see a gap under the wall of flames. He edged closer to investigate. Dotted around the edges of the salt circles were dozens of tiny black hissing holes.

Jarell wrinkled his nose. It was just like when they found a gas leak next door. *What did Tomi say about the sky salt and its illusions?*

Jarell smashed his fist against the ground until lumps of salt broke away. Nozzles. Lots of them. All pumping out gas. This was how Oufula was creating the flames – not magic, but tech. *Use what you can see*, Legsy had said. Now he just needed to figure out how.

As his hand covered a nozzle, the flame directly overhead died. Even so, Jarell decided, he'd need to cover a whole load to make it safely under the wall of fire.

A crack of thunder roared overhead. "The first axe has been claimed!" Oufula announced. "Only two remain."

Jarell bit his lip, trying to psych himself up. He remembered playing soldiers with Lucas when they were smaller and his older brother yelling "Commando style!" at him.

OK, Lucas, just like we practised, Jarell said to himself.

He shot forward under the flames, using his elbows and feet to drag himself across the grainy floor. Gas choked his throat. Sweat stung his eyes.

His arms strained with the effort, but stopping would be deadly.

Suddenly, the heat lessened. He was past the flames!

Jarell stood, gulping down the clean air, and ran on. *Try your worst, Oufula*, Jarell thought, *I'm going to beat your maze and get to an axe next!*

Then he spotted something odd on the ground at the next junction. *Was that a foot?* He sprinted forward with a growing sense of dread. He recognized the scorched uniform. It was *Kimisi*!

CHAPTER EIGHT

THE FINAL THREE

The walls of lightning crackled around Jarell as he crouched beside Kimisi's body. He turned her over. She looked peaceful, as if she was asleep. She was barely breathing.

"Kimisi." Jarell's voice was no more than a whisper. His whole body felt strangely cold. *She had to be OK. Had to be.*

"Kimisi," he said louder, shaking her. "Kimisi!"

Kimisi gasped and her eyes shot open. "Haba, my head hurts like I was just trampled by a herd of Wildebeests."

"Thank the Ancients you're alive," Jarell exhaled. "Did you get caught by the lightning?"

Kimisi sat up. "No, I don't think so. Something else knocked me out," she replied. "This maze is full of tricks, eh?"

Jarell held out a hand and helped her to her feet. Despite grinning at him, her eyes told him that Kimisi was in much more pain than she was letting on. *We have to get out of here before it's too late, but which way?*

There were three options to choose from, but the corridors of lightning were identical. Jarell wasn't even sure which one he had come down. He doubted Kimisi knew either. He looked up, hoping for a clue. The dazzling walls of electricity stretched up high. *Useless.*

Something, a blur, rippled through the wall of lightning. Jarell shook his head. He had been staring into a light too long, that was all.

Except, he suddenly realized, *the shadow of a bright light stayed in the same place*. He vaguely remembered his teacher talking about the eye's cones and rods in science class while he was drawing a picture of the bat-like Asanbosam that he'd fought in the City of Clay.

Jarell blinked and the blur vanished. He looked up again. He could see faint round metallic shapes lining the walls of the corridors. *If the fire were a high-tech trick, why couldn't the sheets of lightning be the same?* Just a giant version of the device his science teacher had used to create sparks during one of their lessons.

He was about to tell Kimisi, when he noticed one of the round blurs swinging down between the walls of the corridor, heading towards them. "Kimisi, we need to go."

"Which way do you—?" Kimisi started as the grey blur stopped overhead.

The air around them thickened with the hum of static electricity. Even his suit couldn't stop the hairs on his arms standing on end.

No time, Jarell realized, knocking Kimisi out of the way and jumping after her.

"What in Ulfrika?" Kimisi yelled.

A giant bolt of lightning smashed into the ground where they had been standing. It left a dark burn mark in the sky salt.

"Don't think that means I owe you," Kimisi said, clearly stunned.

"We're not out of the woods yet," Jarell replied.

"What woods?" Kimisi asked, looking around. "There are no woods in Fekuk. This is a maze, Jarell."

Jarell sighed.

The ground started to hiss around them and a pungent smell filled the air. Kimisi shot him a worried look.

"Quick," Jarell shouted. "Before the gas ignites!"

They scrambled to their feet and sprinted away in the only direction they could.

Whoomph! A fireball exploded behind them. They pelted towards a junction, the fire hot on their heels. They skidded around the corner, then another. The fireball followed them like a homing missile.

"Go right!" Jarell yelled at the next junction.

But just as they were about to turn, a wall of

lightning blocked their exit. "Down," screamed Kimisi. They hit the sky salt as the wave of fire roared over them, then vanished.

"How did it follow us?" Kimisi panted.

Jarell showed her the nozzles hidden in the sky salt and explained about the devices above that generated the walls of lightning.

"Baku, Ayana would not resort to such cheap tricks!" Kimisi said finally.

It didn't matter, they had reached a dead end. "We're going to have to go back," Jarell replied.

"I wouldn't be so sure. Tech is easier to defeat than magic," Kimisi said, fiddling with her gauntlet and holding it up to the wall. "By Ayana's grace, I knew it!" She looked at him and grinned. "I noticed those platforms moving in a pattern. It's the same for this wall of lightning. If you look very carefully, it's flickering."

Jarell's vision blurred slightly as the transparent shades over his eyes darkened, shading out all the colour.

Now, instead of a solid wall of lightning, Jarell could see strips of dark and light dancing. Electric bolts pulsing on and off faster than his brother's beloved strobe light.

"A bigger gap appears every ten seconds," Kimisi said. "Three, two…"

Blink and you could've missed it, Jarell thought. But he had glimpsed what was on the other side. This was the end of the maze. "All we need to do is jump through a wall of lightning. Simple," he muttered.

"It's not simple," Kimisi said. "We have to time it perfectly, or we'll be crisper than a fried kuffcof leaf. Get ready to go when I say."

Jarell braced himself. *Don't think about being fried alive, focus on getting one of the remaining* axes, he told himself. *If Ikala wins, he'll destroy both our worlds. At least Kimisi is jumping with me.*

"Five, four, three..." Kimisi counted down. Jarell could see that slightly bigger gap in the wall hurtling towards them. It was going so fast. No time to—

A shove pitched him into the lightning. It crackled like a ball of plasma and then vanished. He landed heavily on the other side, winded from the fall. Kimisi was nowhere to be seen – she'd pushed him! He was out of the maze, but she was still trapped inside it. *I need to go back for her.*

Suddenly, a clap of thunder shook the stadium, followed by a deep laugh. "Ikala claims the second axe!" Oufula's voice boomed. "Only one axe remains."

Only one place left in the final, Jarell realized.

As he stood, a sly-faced warrior stumbled

through the wall of lightning. He glared at Jarell like a fox caught raiding a bin. Without a second's more hesitation, he sprinted off.

Oh no you don't. Jarell dashed after him. The last axe had to be his.

As much as Jarell lengthened his stride, as hard as his feet pounded the ground and sky salt crunched under his shoes, he was barely gaining on the warrior. There was less than a hundred metres to go. *If only I could use the power of the Iron Leopard,* he thought. *I'd overtake him easily!*

There's more than magic in a staff, Jarell, the voice of Kundi whispered. *This is the land of the ancient-future. To soar with the eagle, one must first learn to stretch their wings.*

The staff doesn't have wings, Jarell thought angrily. *But it does stretch.*

Jarell pulled the staff from his belt loop as he

ran. It was only the size of his hand now, but it could grow to its normal size at the press of a button. *I could use it as pole vault, right?* With enough speed, he'd sail over the other contestant. *Only problem is I've not done that much pole-vaulting.*

Jarell gulped and extended the staff, it grew to four times its normal length at each press of the button.

He jabbed the staff into the ground and kept running.

The pole bent.

"Jump!" Bo-de yelled from the stands. "Let's see you fly!"

Jarell leapt into the air. As the pressure released from the staff, it sprung back straight, lifting Jarell higher and faster. He felt like a bird of prey, swooping over the other contestant.

Jarell spotted the finish line. Ikala was there.

He was surprised to see Tomi there too. At the top of the arc, he twisted his body forward, picking up speed as the ground rushed towards him.

Sky salt sprayed into the air as he hit the ground and tucked into a combat rolling pose. The staff shrunk and tucked away, Jarell bounced to his feet and sprinted as fast as he could. He could hear the other warrior catching up behind him.

Jarell leapt up to the last pillar, catching the axe by the handle. As he landed, the crowd went wild.

"I did it!" Jarell panted.

The other warrior slumped to the ground, exhausted and defeated. Behind him, the maze vanished. And Jarell saw the other two contestants, including Kimisi, being escorted away by the robot guards.

"Cheat!" Ikala complained loudly. "How can this be allowed? Untrustworthy spawn of Kundi. I bet his whole worthless family are cheats!"

Jarell's face burned with anger. He spun around to face Ikala with the axe tightly clenched in his hands. "Leave my family out of it," he spat, stepping closer. "They're better people than you could ever be."

"Careful, Jarell," Tomi said, placing a cool hand on his shoulders. "He wants you to break the rules – if you disrespect the contest, you'll be out."

Jarell glared at him. "The contest?" he huffed. "If I stop Ikala now, this all ends."

"You gave your word," Tomi reminded him. "Trust me. Lower your axe."

Jarell forced himself to relax his grip on the axe and lowered it. He focused on his breathing, using the pull of air in and out of his lungs to calm his mind. *Ikala wants you angry*, he told himself. *Stay calm and focus on winning the Iron Eagle.*

Ikala hissed in frustration. "Why are you so keen to trust this weak-minded *old man*?" Ikala snarled. "What use is a trickster who is so easily tricked?"

A trickster? What did that mean? Jarell wondered.

Tomi let go of Jarell and started towards Ikala.

"ENOUGH!" Oufula thundered. The Ancient soared downwards and stood between them. "Save your energy for the final challenge."

CHAPTER NINE

A DANCE TO THE DEATH

Oufula clicked his fingers.

Jarell found himself suddenly in the middle of the arena. The sky salt had become bare brown earth. Tomi stood some distance away to the right, Ikala to the left. Oufula was back on his throne. Even Tomi looked surprised.

"The rules are simple," Oufula began. "Each

of you has an axe of Fekuk. No other weapons or magic are allowed. It is a dance to the death that only the most graceful and skilful warrior will survive." Jarell didn't need to test the blades to see how sharp they were. He gulped. *Let's hope Ikala and Tomi have no idea how to fight with axes either.*

The ground trembled as a hole opened between the three contestants. *What now?* A tower of whirling metal rose from the middle of the arena. Eight long arms unfurled from the body of the tower, undulating like some nightmare fairground ride. Every inch of them was covered with spinning blades.

Jarell bet all three of them would want to stay as far away from that thing as possible. It looked like death times a million.

"One final thing," Oufula said. "No anti-gravity force fields."

Jarell frowned. Why would they need an anti-gravity force field?

Behind him, the ground cracked like baked clay and began to crumble away. As the gap widened, it curved around towards Tomi and Ikala. It joined up with more cracks, turning the arena into a giant, circular platform. This time nothing would catch them if they fell. It was a long, long drop to the crater below.

Oufula clapped his hands. "Let the entertainment begin!"

Straight away, Tomi made a dash for Ikala. At the same moment, Ikala plunged into the swirling mess of blades. The sorcerer slipped between the deadly arms with ease, his cold stare trained on Jarell before he disappeared from sight.

Jarell took up an Ingalo stance. Weighing the axe in his hand, he wondered how best to use it.

Legsy insisted that true masters of Ingalo didn't need weapons, but while Ikala had one, Jarell wasn't going to take his chances.

Work with what you have, he decided. *Let Ikala make the mistakes.*

The sorcerer broke from the swirling blades. With a terrifying war cry, he threw his axe at Jarell.

Time seemed to slow as the axe spun through the air like a throwing star from one of Lucas's games. Aware of every muscle in his arm, Jarell desperately lifted his axe to block it.

Clang! Ikala's weapon smashed the axe from his hand, sending them both spinning over Jarell's head. They skidded across the ground and over the edge into the crater below. Jarell's heartbeat pounded in his ears. Only Tomi was still armed, but he was walking along the edge of the platform.

Hand-to-hand combat with Ikala. There was no way he could win.

"Meet your end!" Ikala snarled, prowling towards him.

Over the roar of the crowd, Jarell caught Kimisi singing. Her song filled his mind and calmed his body. He smiled. *Everything we have faced seemed impossible, but we have won*, he thought. *This time—*

Ikala exploded forward into the fight. He was fast, and Jarell barely had time to block the series of punches and kicks.

As Jarell fell back, Ikala lunged forward with his next punch. But it only exposed the sorcerer for an attack.

Now! Jarell sprung forward with a kick to Ikala's stomach, followed by a blow to the chest. Ikala grabbed his wrist, then threw him over his shoulder. Jarell rolled as he hit the ground, letting his momentum create some space between him and the sorcerer.

The crowd cheered, but Jarell blocked their shouts out. He needed every ounce of focus to beat Ikala.

Ikala stalked forward, his arms poised ready to strike.

Jarell jumped up, ready for the next round. His heart pounded, his body twitching at even the slightest movement from his opponent.

But a firm push to the side sent Jarell sprawling back to the dirt, mud filling his mouth. "My turn to deal with the sorcerer," Tomi hissed. "You've faced him and his servants too often."

The old man stepped over him to get closer to Ikala and tossed his axe aside.

Ikala laughed and shrugged. "Which order I defeat you in doesn't matter to me."

Jarell scrambled up out of the way, puzzled and thankful for Tomi's help. Why was Tomi helping him? Why would he throw away his axe?

Tomi shifted into a familiar Ingalo stance, his hands and feet angled for attack. Jarell frowned. He'd seen that exact posture somewhere before. *But where?*

Ikala beckoned Tomi closer, but the old man shook his head. "Nice try, Ikala," he said. "I'm not that easy to fool."

Ikala rushed at him, Tomi avoiding slicing blow after slicing blow. The old man was surprisingly fast. Not fast enough, though, to avoid a roundhouse kick to the side. *Smack!* The old man staggered back from the impact, his arm twisting at an unnatural angle. Jarell felt sick to even look at it.

"Too embarrassed to show your true self, *old man*?" Ikala asked.

"You should be embarrassed to call yourself Ulfrikan," Tomi said calmly. "And I am not embarrassed about who I am. My name is Olegu, the trickster god. The God of Doorways."

Jarell blinked in surprise as the old man suddenly transformed into the pencil-thin Legsy, like clay remoulding itself. The crowd gasped. *This can't be true*, Jarell told himself. *Legsy had been banished from Ulfrika, forbidden from ever returning.*

"At last, old friend." The smile on Ikala's face was anything but friendly. "I owe you thanks for freeing me from Kundi's wretched prison."

"You freed Ikala?" Jarell asked, his voice barely above a whisper. As Legsy nodded, Jarell felt weak. All this time, Legsy was the one who had betrayed Ulfrika. "Kimisi was right, you *are* just a trickster. You lied to me."

Legsy hesitated and then took a step towards him, but Jarell scrambled to his feet and ran. He didn't want to let the god talk his way out of this one. *What if Legsy had been getting him to reunite the Staff of Kundi in order to give it to Ikala?* Jarell stopped at the crumbling edge and stared down at the clouds passing under the city. The gap had widened – the area on which they were fighting was getting smaller.

"Jarell, it's not what you think," Legsy shouted

after him. "The truth was just too painful. I should have told you, but I was afraid. I made a mistake. It was cowardly not to tell you—"

"By the gods, cowardly and boring," Ikala snapped. "If I had been in Jarell's shoes, I'd have ended you by now. But I'm going to have to do it myself!"

As Jarell turned, the sorcerer charged at Legsy. He drove his shoulder into the trickster's chest with a grunt. Before he'd even recovered from the blow, Ikala had the trickster's arms twisted behind his back. The Ancient hadn't even attempted to defend himself.

Ikala glanced between the drop and the spinning tower of blades.

"Fight back, Legsy!" Jarell yelled to his own surprise. It had been wrong of Legsy not to tell him the truth, but in his heart Jarell knew Legsy was a good person. "Fight back!"

Legsy shook his head. "I deserve this. You learning the truth was the sacrifice I promised Oufula, but I'm glad you know. Save yourself, Jarell – for your family and for Ulfrika."

The sorcerer laughed at Legsy's words, dragging him towards the whirling mass of blades. Jarell's throat tightened at the unfolding horror. He had to act, but he was frozen to the spot. Legsy deserved better. The Ancient had helped Jarell find a path to his ancestral land. He'd given him Ulfrika and his history and the knowledge that Jarell was descended from a great warrior when all there had been before was absence.

Jarell stopped himself reaching for the staff. Using it to rescue Legsy would disqualify him. Ikala would automatically win the Iron Eagle. *What would Kundi do?*

He squatted down, pressing his hand to the dirt. The city of Fekuk may have been floating, but it was still part of Ulfrika and this was Ulfrikan soil.

"Kundi," he breathed. "How do I save my friend alone?"

In Ulfrika, you're never alone, his ancestor's spirit whispered to him. *A true hero builds on those who came before and will build for those who come after.*

As the ancient spirit flowed into his body, Jarell felt stronger, quicker and braver than ever. As one, Jarell and Kundi could stop Ikala without weapons or magic. Jarell smiled. Ikala was ignoring him to deal with Legsy. *His mistake.*

Jarell sprinted towards Ikala and Legsy, knowing he had the element of surprise on his side.

Ikala's head snapped round. The smug smile fell from his face. "K-Kundi?" he stuttered. "How?"

Jarell stopped and looked down at his hand and saw it was a man's hand and not a child's.

Ikala threw Legsy aside like a rag doll, just missing the spinning blades. The god did not move. "What's the matter, *Ikala*?" Jarell hissed. "Did you not know that the spirit of Kundi lives?"

"I'll show you spirit!" Sliding his hands together, Ikala conjured up a plasma-green coloured ball of energy. He pulled it back and fired.

Jarell dived out of the way just in time. He tucked into a roll and then flipped back on to his feet. He looked down at his hands and they were once again his. *Thank you*, he said silently to Kundi. They had spooked Ikala enough that he had used magic. Now he was disqualified.

Ikala paced away from the blades, drawing more magic into his hands.

"Not fair!" Kimisi yelled from the crowd. "That's against the rules of the contest, Oufula! Ikala is disqualified."

"New rules, little griot," the God of Thunder's voice boomed. "Maybe using their powers will make this fight more interesting! I don't want it to be over yet."

Jarell didn't take his eyes off Ikala. It didn't matter what Oufula decided – he knew what he had to do.

The crowd cheered as Ikala fired more bolts of energy at Jarell.

Jarell managed to outrun the first three explosions, but the fourth sent him tumbling. "Not so brave now," Ikala taunted.

As Jarell got to his feet, he pulled the staff from his belt. "In Ulfrika, we stand up for what is right!" he declared, extending the Staff of Kundi to its full size. The three Iron Animals rippled in support. "Your thirst for power will never prosper, Ikala."

"We'll see about that," Ikala snarled, firing again.

This time Jarell was ready. He struck the staff against the ground and called on the power of the Iron Leopard. Its power surged through him, helping him dodge a barrage of magic from Ikala, but he found himself next to the whirling blades of Oufula's deadly machine.

Summoning the power of the Iron Snake, Jarell drew the earth into a wave that buried the device. A creaking groan came from beneath the mound as the blades stopped whirling, but there was another sound as well.

What felt like an earthquake shook what was left of the floating arena. Bigger chunks of ground started to fall away. *Better finish this soon*, Jarell realized. *Or I might not have ground to stand on.*

He leapt over the remains of Oufula's tower and landed close to Ikala.

The sorcerer whipped a staff out from under his crimson cloak. It was carved with angry-looking symbols that glowed a siren red. He smashed it at Jarell, swiping left and right.

Jarell fought back with the Staff of Kundi, which protected him, guiding his hands to block every blow.

"You delay the inevitable, Jarell," Ikala spat.

A vicious blow caught Jarell and the staff off guard, knocking him to the ground.

"I will rule Ulfrika." The sorcerer raised his staff. "Surrender and I might consider leaving your world alone."

"Never," Jarell wheezed, trying to get his breath back.

Out of nowhere, Legsy crashed into Ikala, knocking the staff from his hands. Legsy used a rolling Ingalo wrestling move to flip Ikala over and over again until they reached the edge of the platform.

"Watch out, Legsy!" yelled Jarell, scrambling to save his friend.

But it was already too late. Legsy and Ikala, still embraced in battle, dropped over the edge.

CHAPTER TEN

HONOUR

Jarell felt he was waking from a dream. A chant of *"champion, champion"* had been taken up by the spectators. He could hear Kimisi and Bo-de cheering the loudest from the stalls where the audience stood. The voices reached him clearly from across the chasm that lay between him and the spectators. Everywhere he looked flags were

being waved and drums beaten with excitement. He'd won, but Legsy... Legsy was gone.

A cold wind chilled the stadium as Oufula stood, extinguishing the celebrations as easily as blowing out a candle. "I decide who is champion!" he bellowed. "This one is not worthy!"

Jarell narrowed his eyes, but Legsy was not there to help him stay calm. Jarell had to be smart all by himself. Somehow he knew that getting into a fight with Oufula in his own city would not go well.

"You betray your honour, Oufula!" Kimisi yelled from the stands. Robot guards were already restraining her and Bo-de. "Jarell is worthy."

"Yeah," Bo-de chipped in. "He might be skinny, but he did win your contest."

A clap of thunder echoed around the arena. "Quiet," Oufula growled. He let lightning dance between his fingers.

"I've earned the right to speak. It is my destiny to reunite all four Iron Animals on to the Staff of Kundi," Jarell declared. "I know you're angry at Ayana, but going back on your word won't help you win her back!"

Oufula laughed dryly. "Who said I want her back? Besides, I have grown fond of the Iron Eagle. Ayana can come and take it away from me personally if she wants."

As Oufula mentioned the storm goddess, the wind picked up and the skies darkened. Jarell felt hope rise in his chest. Ayana had helped him and Kimisi at the start of his quest, would she help him now that he was so close to completing it?

Oufula's laugh shook the stadium like thunder. "Oh, poor boy, you thought she was coming, didn't you?" The bird on Oufula's shoulder flapped its wings and gave an ear-piercing screech. The God of Thunder reached up and soothed it. "As I've learned," Oufula said, "Ayana only appears when it suits her. Now, you can leave my city quietly – or painfully – but the Iron Eagle stays with me."

Jarell swallowed; he had made a promise to reunite the staff with its animals. He had one more card to play. *If Ayana won't come to me, perhaps the Iron Eagle will*, he thought. Each Iron Animal had strengthened the staff's connection with the others. He struck the Staff of Kundi against the ground three times to awaken the animals' powers.

Help me find your friend, he told them.

The leopard's ears pricked up listening for the eagle. The snake's tongue flickered in the air. Jarell remembered that that was how snakes smelled. The crocodile waited and then all three roared together.

Nothing.

Oufula clapped, slowly and loudly. "The Future Hero clearly thinks crows have eaten my brain," he said. "The first thing I did was hide the Iron Eagle. Otherwise Ikala would have tried to snatch it from me. Never trust a sorcerer."

"A wise or daring move," a cold voice added behind Jarell.

Jarell spun around to meet Ikala's devious smile.

He survived the drop! Has Legsy survived too?

"I concede, Oufula, you hid the eagle well if even the other Iron Animals can't find it," Ikala continued. "But the trickster god is gone. The game is over. It is time I got my prize."

Ikala swept past Jarell and addressed the whole stadium. "How long has Ulfrika waited for a leader to unite us?" he asked, his voice suddenly amplified so it easily crossed the chasm that surrounded the battleground where Jarell and Ikala stood. "With the staff I can be that leader. Unlike Jarell, I am a true warrior and a true Ulfrikan! Unlike Oufula, who sits here licking his wounds because he is no longer loved." The God of Thunder narrowed his eyes but said nothing. "It is time for change. Ulfrika could be the greatest kingdom in all the universes."

A murmur of agreement went through the crowd. *What if Ikala wins them over?*

"Don't listen to him!" Jarell objected. "Ulfrika

thrives. Ikala would have you fight others. He would have you forget who you really are."

Ikala sighed and turned to him. "Surrender and I will let you return to your true home," he said. "My people deserve to be led by one of their own."

"Jarell *is* one of our own!" Kimisi vaulted into the centre of the arena using her spear. She reached Jarell's side with her spear already charged. "And he's brave! We've defeated every challenge you've thrown at us."

"It's two against one, Ikala," Jarell said. "I like our odds."

"Is that so?" Ikala purred.

Were-hyena howls rose up. Jarell turned to see them pull themselves up on to the battleground and bound over to Ikala. They thumped their furry chests as their long fangs dripped with spit. Dark shadows swooped across the army-grey skies.

Jarell's skin crawled as the Asanbosams' blood-red eyes stared back at him, the flapping sound of their dusky bat-like wings like vicious whips. Moments later, two dozen giant scorpions appeared in the stands and leapt into the battleground. An eerie light poured from the Asanbosams' eyes, and then the scorpions' eyes began glowing too.

Zonby scorpions! Jarell remembered the Asanbosams' power to make zombie-like creatures out of anyone. They would now do anything the Asanbosams commanded.

"No Placid Boomslangs or Zin, then?" Jarell asked, recalling the other creatures Ikala had sent against him during his last quests. He tried to sound brave, but his voice still cracked with fear. Even Kimisi looked worried.

"Now *this* is more like it!" Oufula boomed as he landed between him and Ikala. His eyes burned

bright with excitement. "Some real fun at last!"

Fiery battle axes appeared in Oufula's hand.

The members of the audience who hadn't already fled the display applauded. He acknowledged them with a slight bow.

"Pick a side, Oufula," Ikala said. "This *runt* descended from a half forgotten annoyance, or a real leader? You have no interest in ruling Ulfrika, so I will leave your kingdom alone. I can make you more powerful than ever! And think how such an alliance would enrage Ayana."

Oufula smirked. "A promising proposal, sorcerer. Shall we ask the *runt* what he has to offer?"

Kimisi turned to Jarell, but he shook his head. Oufula was never going to side with them.

Kimisi stepped closer to Oufula and cleared her throat. "Oufula, God of Thunder, with all respect.

There is an old saying: love sways like grass in the wind until it is broken. Ayana says she doesn't love you, but she still trusts you – she sent *you* the Iron Eagle. Break her trust and there may be no going back."

Jarell watched Oufula's reaction, expecting him to fly into a rage. The flashy god hesitated and turned to face the bird perched on his shoulder. It stopped preening its coppery feathers and looked at him.

"Which path would you choose?" Oufula asked it.

Casting its beady eyes over Jarell and Ikala, the bird returned its gaze to Oufula. It screeched into his ear.

Oufula bowed his head. "A good decision, my beauty. Now fly."

Gracefully, Oufula's bird launched itself into the

air. As it beat its massive wings, coppery feathers fell like confetti. It soared and spun, a ball of sky-blue lightning gathering around it. *It's changing*, Jarell realized.

In a burst of light, the giant bird was gone and the Iron Eagle was there, twirling in the air. A bird made of metal but also alive. *It was right here in front of us all this time.*

Jarell shook his head at Oufula's audacity and cleverness.

"That bird is mine!" Ikala shouted.

The Iron Eagle turned sharply as something shadowy tried to grasp it. Ikala had conjured up two columns of thick smoke that he was controlling with his arms. They swiped and snatched at the Iron Eagle, trying to seize it by force.

"Jarell, do something!" Kimisi yelled. "Before Ikala captures it!"

Jarell raised the staff, but stopped. If he used his powers to capture the eagle, he would be just like Ikala – taking and not asking. Closing his eyes, Jarell reached out with his mind to the bird. *Zura Mohlo, great Iron Eagle*, he told it. *We need you. Will you come?*

The eagle screeched and Jarell opened his eyes. It swooped towards him. He held up the staff and dipped his head in thanks. The Iron Eagle had chosen. The bird soared over his shoulder, disappearing into the dark clouds above.

"Baku!" Kimisi muttered. "Why are animals so annoying."

"It is the eagle's choice," Jarell whispered, watching what Ikala was going to do next. "We must respect it."

Kimisi sighed. "It was always said that the animals offered themselves to Kundi. Perhaps that is why their power was always strongest when Kundi wielded the staff."

"So the eagle's wise enough to want nothing to do with the Future Hero," Ikala taunted. "Without a completed staff, you shall be easy to defeat!"

A piercing shriek above made everyone look

up. The Iron Eagle was plunging back towards them. Instantly, Ikala sent smoke pouring after the eagle. It swooped and dodged as Ikala tried to ensnare it again.

The Staff of Kundi burned like a beacon with golden light. Jarell held it up high, ready to welcome home the last Iron Animal. The eagle landed atop the staff in a blaze of sky-blue light.

The staff thrummed with an ancient power far stronger than anything Jarell had experienced in all his time in Ulfrika.

It felt as if all of his senses were amplified. He could hear a pin drop. He could smell the sweat and thirst for power on Ikala.

So this was what Kundi was working with, Jarell thought. No wonder he was the greatest warrior Ulfrika had ever seen. His ancestor.

"Sides have been chosen and war begins," Ikala snarled. Suddenly, Jarell noticed Oufula standing next to Kimisi, battle axes ready.

"War," Jarell muttered. Where was his vast army like those in the stories of Kundi that Kimisi had told him? Even with the God of Thunder and Kimisi, their side was badly outnumbered by giant scorpions, Asanbosam and Were-hyenas.

Then, suddenly, everything slowed. A mist appeared in front of him like an autumn morning in London. From the fog, a ghostly figure appeared.

Aside from the gold breastplate, it could

have been a member of his family from the barbershop. It could be Uncle Malcolm. The man had his dad's serious expression when something important needed to be discussed. The shape of his eyes were just like Lucas's. But this was not a living person, he could tell from the transparency of his skin. This was the spirit of his ancestor – Ulfrika's greatest king.

Jarell put his fists together and pressed them to his chest. "Zura Mohlo."

Kundi returned the greeting with his ghostly hands. *True Ulfrikans always hear the call of the eagle*, his ancestor's voice echoed in his mind.

Jarell's throat felt too dry to speak. He wondered how far the cry of the eagle could be heard – and who would answer it for him? He gripped the staff tightly and summoned the power of the Iron Eagle. *Help me get word to my friends*, he told it.

The Iron Eagle glowed with the brilliance of a cloudless sky. The next moment Jarell was high above Fekuk. He no longer had a physical body, but a weightless spirit body that flew alongside the eagle and Kundi.

The eagle whistled. Suddenly, they were over Ayana's vast temple grounds and all the reflecting pools. Another whistle, and below them stretched the colourful shifting sands of the Muho Desert, then the volcanic lands of Ekpani, then the glistening turquoise of Tekanu's lake and then the scrubland surrounding the cities of Sila and Keesah. *This is what we fight for, the wonders of Ulfrika.*

"It is time," Kundi said. With the Iron Eagle's earth-shuddering screech, Jarell was in his body back in the arena. Kundi's ghostly golden form stood beside him. *We fight.*

Robot and human soldiers were marching into the arena, taking up positions behind him. The Asanbosam moved the giant Zonby scorpions to face them, while Were-hyenas crept closer.

"Leave Jarell for Ikala!" the Were-hyena leader, Baraz, snarled to his followers.

Jarell recognized him from his unique cloak,

pelted with Were-hyena prey. "And leave the griot for me!"

Jarell's eyes narrowed at the sorcerer rubbing his gauntleted hands together. Kimisi, Oufula and his army would only need to fight as long as Ikala remained in charge. Take out Ikala, Jarell realized, and his forces would crumble.

CHAPTER ELEVEN

WAR

Jarell glanced over the almost empty stands and spotted the eight warriors from the contest. "Join me," he called. "Save Ulrika from Ikala and I will get Oufula to give you back what you pledged to join the contest."

Even Afidi the Mighty grinned as the warriors readied their weapons and vaulted into the arena to join the soldiers and robot guards of Fekuk.

"We will discuss that promise after the battle, Future Hero," Oufula said. "I—"

Before he could finish, Ikala fired at them. Jarell dived to the ground, just missing the blast. He scrambled up and raised the staff. "For Ulfrika!" he yelled and the battle began.

Packs of Were-hyenas and giant scorpions surged forward, smashing into the orderly rows of Fekuk's soldiers. Kimisi ran over to help Afidi and the other warriors. Oufula waded through enemy lines, swinging his axes and raining lightning down on Ikala. But the sorcerer deflected it with ease using the plasma shield on his forearm. Ikala then returned fire with his own blasts of magic. Stray bolts exploded against the stands and the city around them.

Something dark flitted in the air above him. Jarell ducked just in time to escape the metal talons of an Asanbosam. He sent a blast after it, before a pack of snarling Were-hyenas lunged for him.

Jarell slipped into an Ingalo stance, knocking aside the first two creatures and then driving the staff into another's stomach. Using the staff as leverage, he spun around as two more tried to claw him. He hit back by smashing the staff against their wrinkled snouts.

The creatures fell back whimpering. Jarell tried to catch his breath. Everywhere he looked his people were locked in furious battles with Ikala's forces. Even in the stands, Bo-de was riding on the shoulders of a robot guard and shouting orders in a battle against a small pack of Were-hyenas. Bo-de cheered as his soldiers tossed one to the ground.

A blast from either Ikala or Oufula smashed into the buildings overhead. A chunk of stone and high-tech metal crashed down. The whole arena shook from the impact. Several scorpions tried to flee but the Asanbosam brought them back under control.

Jarell refocused his attention on Ikala. He and Oufula were battling it out at the far end of the stadium. Their blasts were causing more damage to the city than each other. He raised up the staff and aimed it at Ikala.

Now. A lava-red bolt shot from the staff over the battling soldiers and guards, Were-hyenas and scorpions. It missed Ikala and exploded against a pillar behind him, shaking the whole city.

"Baku," Jarell said under his breath. "I need to get closer."

He had just run forward when a sharp cry from

Kimisi stopped him in his tracks. She was with Afidi leading a mix of Oufula's robot and human guards. Giant desert scorpions surrounded them on all sides.

As Jarell sprinted towards them, Asanbosam glided over the group. Within seconds, many of Fekuk's human soldiers had stopped fighting. Their eyes blazed with an eerie white light. "Zonby!" Kimisi yelled. "Push them out!"

"Almost with you, Kimisi," Jarell yelled.

But before he could take another step, a group of six giant scorpions scuttled in front of him. Each as big as an SUV, stalking towards him as one. Their pincers snapped hungrily and their massive emerald tails were raised high, ready to strike.

Jarell slammed the Staff of Kundi into the ground and called on the power of the Iron

Leopard. *Do your thing*, Jarell shouted to it as he pointed the staff at the creatures.

Jets of fire erupted from the staff like a flamethrower at the line of scorpions, but it did nothing to slow them down. Instead, several throbbing stingers darted at him.

Jarell jumped back. He took a deep breath and focused on the power of the Iron Crocodile. Its eyes glowed a dark green and pools of water gathered on the sky salt under the scorpions. The creatures managed a few splashing steps before the pools became a wave of water that lifted them up. But they fought against the flood, their claws digging into the stadium floor.

As the water receded, just two of the scorpions had been washed away. More came to take their place. The snap of pincers forced him back again.

"Not fire, nor water. Maybe this then," Jarell

whispered, calling on the power of the Iron Snake. Its eyes glowed with a reddish-brown light and the pearl in its mouth sparkled. It slipped down the staff and touched the sky salt.

Instantly, giant claws of mud burst from the floor. They towered into the air and smashed down on to the scorpions like massive fists. The scorpions fought as they were dragged down by the soil and rock.

For a split second, Jarell thought he had beaten them. But then the earth started shaking as the scorpions clawed their way back on to the surface, their stingers pulsing more furiously than ever, and darted after him. They were fast, but the power of the Iron Leopard made him faster. As he dodged poisoned stingers and snapping pincers, they pushed him back. He was losing ground.

Jarell stumbled up the steps to Oufula's throne.

They've almost got me cornered, he realized as he clambered up higher.

He glanced at the Iron Eagle. "You're my last hope," he said. "Don't let me down!"

Jarell called on the power of the Iron Eagle. Its eyes burned sky blue as it let out a low whistling call. A wind snatched at the scorpions, ripping their claws from the ground. Jarell spun them in the air with the staff and sent them flying over the stadium walls.

Panting, he noticed the broken robot guards littering the arena. Even the once sleek city of Fekuk was beginning to crumble. *Ikala's dividing our forces and ripping them apart*, Jarell realized. It was going to take a miracle to win. *If I can get to Kimisi, perhaps we can rally everyone together. It might be our only chance.*

Jarell leapt down from Oufula's throne and

sprinted towards where Kimisi was fighting. He didn't notice the Asanbosam until it was too late. *Slam!* The winged creature smashed into him, sending him tumbling. The Staff of Kundi fell from his grasp. "No!"

Before Jarell could get it back, more scorpions surrounded him.

Their horrible tiny eyes blazed with white light. The scorpions' tails twitched with anticipation, looming over him ready to strike. He was close enough to see the pulse of radioactive-green venom under the stingers' transparent skin.

Jarell gulped. His staff was just out of reach. *Is this how it ends?*

A strange groan rose from deep within the city, but Jarell was too focused on the stinger darting towards him. Suddenly, the whole stadium lurched sideways as if it were a platform from the first challenge. He rolled with it and the stinger missed.

Venom splashed against the sky salt. It hissed and bubbled, dissolving everything it touched.

Jarell scrambled after the staff, but a scorpion caught him first.

"Get off me!" Jarell yelled, trying to break free of the pincers. "Help!"

With a howl, a Painted Wolf crashed into the scorpion. It bit down on the creature's tail, severing the stinger. The white light from the scorpion's eyes vanished. It threw Jarell aside and turned to fight the creature attacking it.

Jarell rolled as he landed and grabbed the Staff of Kundi.

More howls of Painted Wolves filled the air as hundreds bounded into the stadium. The largest one sprinted to him, leaping over the enemy as if they were just obstacles in a dog show. It stopped in front of Jarell. It flashed a toothy grin.

"Chinell!" Jarell exclaimed.

Chinell bowed. "I told you we would meet again," he said. "My pack and I are at your command, heir of Kundi."

"As are our forces." Tekanu landed in front of them. The blue-robed River Mother pressed her fists against her chest. "The Iron Eagle called, we came."

Another woman landed next to her dressed in a red-and-black pleated robe. Without thinking, Jarell knelt before Ayana, the Goddess of Storms and Rains.

Ayana laughed and Tekanu scowled.

"Stand, Future Hero," Ayana announced. "You summoned Ulfrika to your aid. You served your homeland; now it is our turn."

Jarell saw Ayana's temple guards and Tekanu's merpeople marching into the stadium. The same feeling he had when his whole family had admired his drawing at Uncle Malcolm's party welled up inside him. He had achieved more than he could have imagined – not just reuniting the Staff of Kundi, but all of Ulfrika.

Jarell held out the staff to Ayana. "You can wield it better than me."

Ayana shook her head. "It serves you, heir of Kundi. You have forged it into a new weapon, one that will help only you defeat Ikala."

"Enough yapping," Chinell barked, leaping at the giant scorpions heading their way

The city tilted again, throwing them all to the ground. A building collapsed into the stands, sending up a cloud of dust.

"Fekuk is getting destroyed," Jarell said.

Dozens of scorpions pressed closer.

Ayana's and Tekanu's eyes clouded over. Water swelled from the ground behind the scorpions and thick storm clouds formed above pelting them with rain.

The scorpions dug down against the flash flood.

Realizing what the goddesses were doing, Jarell thrust the Staff of Kundi into the ground. He summoned the power of the Iron Crocodile and the flood became a torrent. It swept up everything in its path, scorpions and Painted Wolves alike! The wolves swam hard, but the current was too strong.

"Save them!" Chinell pleaded.

Jarell called on the power of the Iron Snake. As it touched the ground, great serpents of mud burst from the sky salt. They smashed through the water, scooping up the wolves and lifting them to safety. Chinell raced around making sure each one was OK.

With the scorpions gone, the flood vanished as magically as it had appeared.

Fekuk shuddered again, plunging like a roller coaster. The wall of the enormous crater become visible through the high-tech buildings and gardens. "The city is falling!" Jarell shouted.

Ayana and Tekanu took to the air. "Leave that to us, Future Hero," they said as one, before soaring off under the city.

Even with reinforcements, the battle was far from over. Were-hyenas had Kimisi, Afidi and his fellow warriors cornered. Bo-de was down to just three robot guards. Ayana's guards and Tekanu's merpeople were fighting towards them, but were slowed as the Asanbosam turned many to Zonby.

Even Oufula was struggling under the weight

of Were-hyenas. They clung to him, snapping at his neck. The God of Thunder roared with laughter as if they were simply trying to tickle him, but a full-strength Oufula would have flicked them off like flies.

Jarell glanced at Chinell. "Ready?"

With a curt nod, Jarell and the Painted Wolves charged into battle. Chinell howled. "For Ulfrika! For Jarell!"

CHAPTER TWELVE

JUST LIKE THE OLD TALES

The Painted Wolves smashed into the Were-hyenas, flattening them against the ground. Jarell leapt over the wrestling animals, striking at the legs, chests and wrinkled snouts of the enemy. Were-hyena howls of pain joined the Painted Wolves howls of excitement.

"Kimisi!" Jarell yelled. "We're coming."

"You!" Baraz said, turning around. "And the dogs."

Baraz raked at him with his claws. Jarell dodged them and struck out with the staff. It smashed into the Were-hyena's face. Baraz whimpered as he looked at all four iron animals and fled. With their leader deserting, the other Were-hyenas scarpered too. Painted Wolves and the freed warriors surged after them. Kimisi strode towards Jarell and the leader of the Painted Wolves.

"Took your time, eh," Kimisi said, grinning at Jarell, then winked at Chinell. "And you brought the ungrateful wolf!"

"Jarell," a Painted Wolf interrupted. "Trouble behind you!"

Jarell spun around. Merpeople and Ayana's guards were heading towards them, their spears raised ready to attack. Their eyes glowed brighter than the time Lucas bleached his hair.

"More Zonby!" Jarell exclaimed. "Don't hurt them, hold them back. I'll take care of the Asanbosam."

He kicked the Staff of Kundi into a firing position and called on the power of the Iron Leopard. He fired at the flying beasts, but they flew swiftly, letting energy blasts sail harmlessly behind them.

Kimisi and the wolves were trying their best to bring down the Zonby without injuring them, but the longer they fought the harder it would get.

Jarell focused on the Asanbosam. His blasts needed to be timed perfectly. He took a deep breath. One swooped high above him, and Jarell aimed just ahead of it. *Now!*

POW! The Asanbosam crashed against the sky salt with a satisfying smack. Jarell fired again, striking more of the flying beasts. With a screech, the Asanbosam whirled around and flew out of the city, straight into a torrential rainstorm that had sprung up unexpectedly and sent many of them crashing into the water below.

Ayana and Tekanu's work, Jarell realized straight away. Fekuk was no longer tilting violently, but instead swaying gently like a boat in calm water.

As the Goddess of Storms and the River Mother returned, he thanked them for flooding the crater to save the city.

Across the stadium, merpeople and Ayana's guards were tending to the injured among the wolves and soldiers.

"Who'd have thought you'd beat all those baddies?" Bo-de said as he rolled up on the back of a robot guard.

"There is one more battle to win," Ayana said, pointing. "Ikala!"

The evil sorcerer stood alone. Shattered remains of buildings and robots littered the ground around him. Jarell could picture Ikala turning every world he ruled into rubble. "It's time to finish this."

As Jarell stepped towards the sorcerer, Kimisi joined him.

He stopped and looked at her. He tried to give her a reassuring smile, but she didn't understand. "Kimisi, I have to face Ikala alone," he said softly.

"But we've always fought together," Kimisi replied, frowning.

Ayana placed her hand on Kimisi's shoulder. "Trust the heir of Kundi, Kimisi. This is his task."

Kimisi bit her lip, then nodded. "Just like the old tales," she whispered.

Jarell set off again, completely alone this time.

No, not completely alone, he realized. He felt the reassuring presence of his ancestor Kundi with him. A cold shiver chilled his spine as he caught Ikala's cold dead eyes.

Jarell stopped. Too nervous to speak, he slipped into an Ingalo stance. The air shimmered beside him and the translucent golden spirit of Kundi appeared. *The past and the future together as one*, his ancestor's voice whispered.

Two long, flaming swords appeared in Ikala's hands. "How dare you think you can defeat me!" he snarled. "A runt that has no right to call anywhere home!"

Jarell let Ikala's words wash over him. He was not going to be tricked like Ayana with the sorcerer's misdirection. He spotted his shadow sneaking away. The golden form of Kundi moved towards it. *I'll take care of his shadow.*

"Now give me back what should be mine!" Ikala yelled.

The sorcerer charged. His swords smashing down on the Staff of Kundi as Jarell blocked his moves. Even though Ikala fought fiercely, Jarell caught every blow with the staff.

Suddenly, Ikala swept one of the swords against the ground and flicked a cloud of dust and sky salt into his eyes. Jarell stumbled back, blinking back the tears.

Ikala kicked him against the chest and sent him sprawling across the shattered stone. The swords crackled with power as he pointed them at Jarell.

Jarell spotted Kundi's spirit pinned down by Ikala's shadow, the golden form struggling to get free.

"Like Kundi, you're weak and a coward," Ikala said softly.

He fired.

The Iron Snake darted out and used its pearl orb to absorb the blast. The staff buzzed as if it might explode! Jarell flicked the bolt of energy back at the sorcerer.

Ikala caught the blasts with his swords, but the force knocked him backwards.

As Jarell stood, a burning pain flashed against the back of his head. The winged symbol was reminding him it was time to go home. *No, not now*, Jarell panicked. *I have to end this.*

Ignoring the pain, Jarell banged the Staff of Kundi against the sky salt. "Iron Animals!" he shouted. "For Ulfrika!"

Golden light raced up the metal, changing colour as it touched each animal: a lava red for the Iron Leopard, deep emerald green for the Iron Crocodile, burnt sienna for the Iron Snake and then sky blue for the Iron Eagle. The staff thrummed with power. Its metallic rainbow light surrounded Jarell like armour.

Ikala swept the swords together and fired. The blast crashed into Jarell with all the force of a truck. It smashed against his protective armour, making it glow red-hot. Jarell tried to fight back, but the power was too intense. It held the staff firmly, getting hotter and hotter. Sweat poured from him. *Can the armour hold much longer?*

Then he spotted the snake's pearl orb. It was getting larger, absorbing all the power from Ikala! Jarell swung the staff at the sorcerer. "Surrender," he said.

Ikala hesitated. His eyes narrowed as he stared at the snake's pearl orb.

"You know you are beaten," Jarell said. "Give up and I won't have to use the staff on you."

"I will never give up," the sorcerer spat and plunged the swords into the ground.

In a blaze of sparks, Ikala was gone.

Jarell fell to his knees. He touched the staff to the sky salt and gratefully returned the energy to the Ulfrikan soil. "Thank you," he whispered to the Iron Animals.

Bo-de and Kimisi sprinted over to him.

"Ikala's got some neat tricks," Bo-de said with awe. "But terrible manners. He didn't say goodbye."

As Kimisi laughed, the golden spirit of Jarell's ancestor Kundi came towards him.

What you choose to do next will determine the fate of Ulfrika, Kundi said, fading away. *Choose wisely.*

"Chinell," Jarell called to the leader of the Painted Wolves. "Ikala mustn't get away. Can you track his scent? He probably just cloudported somewhere nearby."

"If he is on land, we will find him," Chinell barked and bounded off with his pack.

Tekanu ordered her merpeople into the lake around Fekuk. "My warriors will search the water," she added.

Jarell nodded. *What other choices do I need to make?* he wondered. *Kundi made it sound like there was a difficult decision ahead.*

The injured were already being taken care of. Not far away from them Ayana nursed the beaten Oufula. Kimisi scowled at Ayana. "How can she help him after all he has done?"

With a gentle breeze, Ayana wafted to Kimisi's side. "Did Oufula not fight at our side?" she asked. "I know he has done wrong, but he deserves kindness too."

Kimisi bowed to the goddess. "Well... Yes..."

Oufula looked up at Jarell and grinned. "So

what will you do now, young hero? Will you rule over Ulfrika with the staff?"

The choice Kundi was talking about, Jarell realized. But before he could answer, the pattern in Jarell's hair flared with pain. It was time to return home.

"Ulfrika is part of me," he answered. "But where my family and friends are … that is also home."

Oufula nodded. "Who will protect Ulfrika then? Me? Ayana?"

Jarell took in the faces of Oufula, Ayana, Tekanu and Chinell. "Only all of you together can stand up against evil such as Ikala." He held out the Staff of Kundi. "This shouldn't be Ayana's to guard alone. Will you protect it with her as one?"

"We will take care of it … *together*," Ayana said taking the staff from him as the other Ancients and Chinell nodded.

Jarell's chest swelled with pride. It felt like the right decision. "One last thing. Oufula, the fees you collected from the contestants, I ask that you return them all but one – *Ikala's*."

"Done!" Oufula grinned. "His second best weapon is now mine!"

Pain lanced through Jarrel's head, as the symbol in his hair burned fiercely.

"Jarell, you must go before it's too late," Kimisi said. She guided him to the water's edge, where Tekanu conjured the portal back to the VIP room at the barbershop.

"Thank you," Jarell said.

Kimisi stared at the view with fascination. "Eh, what a strange world you come from," she remarked. "Will you ever be able to come back?"

"I don't know. With Legsy gone I—" Jarell broke off. It was too painful to think that Legsy was gone. It was too painful to think that he'd never be able to come back to Ulfrika

"You'd better find a way," Kimisi replied. "Either you come back to visit or else I will have to come and visit you. And I'll bring my cousin with me. Not that I know where she is. "

Jarell laughed. "I'm sure my family would love to meet you," he replied. "Take care, Kimisi."

He dived into the magical portal. Darkness surrounded him and he fell through the abyss on to the barbershop floor.

"Welcome back, Future Hero!"

Jarell scrambled up in surprise. "Legsy!" he gasped. "But you— I saw you— How are you alive?"

Legsy grinned as he got up from his barber's chair. "How could I have been in Ulfrika, I was banished, remember? The council of Ancients have not changed their minds about that as far as I can tell."

"But I saw you," Jarell said, blinking back the tears.

Legsy held out a small clay figure that looked just like Tomi. "You saw this."

Jarell's eyes darted to the empty jars on the counter. They had been filled with the clay Jarell brought back from the underground city of Keesah. Legsy nodded.

"Ancient kings once used this clay to send messages great distances," he explained. "I— How do you say it in this world? I upgraded it with a little magic. By shaping

Tomi here, I created a proxy in Ulfrika that I could control and speak through." Legsy held the figure out to Jarell. "I have no use for it now Tomi is gone. Take it to remember your victory."

Jarell took the small clay figure. "Thank you, Legsy," he said. "I vow to help you return to Ulfr—"

The rattle of the beaded curtain cut him off. As Omari popped his head through, the sounds of the party flooded the quiet VIP room.

"No time for trims, cuz!" Omari yelled over the beat of one of Jarell's favourite party songs. "We need to teach Legsy our family's famous electric slide!"

Like I've not already done enough sliding about today, Jarell thought.

Legsy laughed and followed Omari out. "How about it, Jarell? Time to join the celebrations?"

Jarell smiled. There was plenty to celebrate.

THE END

LEGEND
OF THE
FUTURE
HERO

Kundi was the finest hero to ever live in the land of Ulfrika.
He was famed for his powers of healing, he loved to study the
wildlife and found a rich gold mine in the Muho Desert and
shared his wealth.

Ikala was an evil sorcerer who wanted to rule all of Ulfrika
with an iron fist. Kundi defeated Ikala years ago, but Ikala
and his army were so powerful, Kundi had to gather allies
from every corner of Ulfrika to have a chance of winning.
And even then, he was only able to imprison Ikala.

Over the years, Kundi's descendants travelled the realms,
including to our world, leaving the Staff of Kundi, a powerful
weapon, in the safe hands of the Goddess Ayana.

After centuries of plotting and planning, Ikala managed to break free using trickery. He came to the temple of Ayana to get the Staff of Kundi, the only weapon that could defeat him. But the Goddess Ayana split the staff into pieces, spreading its four Iron Animal heads — leopard, eagle, crocodile, snake — across the country using storm magic.

Now Ulfrika waits for the prophesized Future Hero, the Heir of Kundi, to return to their realm as he is the only person who can defeat Ikala with the Staff of Kundi. But first he must find the Iron Animals before Ikala does and reassemble the Staff. Otherwise, Ikala will take over Ulfrika and then begin to seek out new worlds to rule, including ours. . .

Once Jarell was identified as the Future Hero, he travelled to Ulfrika and found the Iron Leopard at Fire Mountain with the help of his warrior-friend Kimisi.

PLACES
IN ULFRIKA

FEKUK

High in the sky, suspended above a volcanic crater, lies the fabled city of Fekuk.

From below, Fekuk looks like a hovering ball of silver spikes. Tall angular skyscrapers reach out from the centre of the city in every direction, with mysterious Ulfrikan symbols carved into the gleaming buildings. Tangled vines hang from star-shaped balconies, and more plants weave across the bridges that connect one building to the next.

To reach Fekuk, Jarell must blow a marsa flute to call for transport. Fekuk's ships look like see-through orbs and are operated by mechanical robot soldiers. Pulsing lights flow over the buildings of Fekuk, hinting at the protective force field placed over the city by the God of Thunder, Oufula.

Oufula is offering the Iron Eagle, the last Iron Animal needed to complete the Staff of Kundi, as the grand prize in a deadly competition he is hosting in Fekuk's enormous sky stadium.